a novel

LOVE unfulfilled

DARRENCE WOLFE

TATE PUBLISHING *& Enterprises*

Love Unfulfilled

Published by Tate Publishing & Enterprises, LLC
127 E. Trade Center Terrace | Mustang, Oklahoma 73064 USA
1.888.361.9473 | www.tatepublishing.com

Tate Publishing is committed to excellence in the publishing industry. The company reflects the philosophy established by the founders, based on Psalm 68:11,
"The Lord gave the word and great was the company of those who published it."

Cover design by Kellie Southerland
Interior design by Stefanie Rooney

Published in the United States of America

ISBN: 978-1-61566-255-5
1. Fiction, African American, Christian
2. Fiction, Christian, Romance
09.11.11

DEDICATION

First, I have to give thanks and praise to God the Father, who is the head of my life, and Jesus Christ, who is my Lord and Savior, and the Holy Spirit for keeping me and guiding me, for without the power and inspiration of God, I would be nothing. This book is dedicated to my loving and devoted wife and my muse, Timeka, of fourteen-plus years, who has been the right rib in my life and not a spare rib, the one who has stood beside me and prayed for me and success to come my way. She is a woman of elegance, grace, and beauty, along with great virtue, who has chiseled me into the man of God I am today through prayer, undying love, and affection to me and our family, praying always that purpose and destiny would overtake our lives and our relationship, positioning us for God's promises. I thank my mom, Lowistine Moton, for giving me life, instruction, and loving me as a mother loves her son, loving her children without limits or strings attached. I thank the Lord for the children he has given me: Breuna, my firstborn, chosen by God for an awesome purpose as well; Sarai, my princess, named through the inspiration of the Lord who continually shows beauty, love, and purity in everything she does; and Joshua, my "little man" who is strong and loving and continues to stand in my stead when I'm not home, out to sea for the navy on deployment. I hope and pray I always make them proud and inspire them to go beyond what I have accomplished. I love you. To Mr. Terrence Miller, creator and founder of the T-Millz Stage Productions, thank you for the inspiration to write again, allowing me to help write *I Told the Storm* and this book. I thank you, son, from the bottom of my heart.

INSPIRATIONAL POEM

"The Prayer of a Single Woman"

A single woman's prayer, can't you see?
It's not filled with dreams but desires and necessities,
Days proved with promise, and future full of purpose,
What a woman wants and what a woman needs is one man
Who can fill every need, in tune with
this lovely lady's heartbeat.
The prayer that she has given has been seasoned with details,
Of love, even cautious intelligent
thought of a strong foundation,
A prayer of careful instruction of the man's love for her,
Knowing that she is the only one for him,
Fitted so jointly together,
Like flesh and bone that has been so finely crafted together,
By God's design, that she should be one with the head,
Knowing that her covering is sure,
She is loved as Christ loved the church
to where he gave his life,
Yearning for true companionship that only God can give,
Down on her knees this supplication is given,
Not to be sanctified and suffering for the love of man.
Love can only be found in the Lord and
down inside of this creation
Falling in love with the God inside of the man.

Written by Darrence A. Wolfe

PREFACE

What do we look for in life most of the time? That someone special from God, the person to share space and time with for the rest of our lives, the one to complete us in our very existence or witness in the wayward walk down here on this very planet. I would like to talk about someone who is looking for this very thing, but because of what life circumstances have dealt and taught this person, and each and every one of us out there, she continues to sample and try before she buys. Despite the prayer that was prayed and the foundation laid, we start losing our target and focus, doing our own thing.

What if you were to pray that very fervent, sincere prayer and ask the Lord for that someone special? Is that so hard to do or impossible for the God that we serve to take care of? For the Bible tells us, "Whoso findeth a wife; findeth a good thing and obtaineth favour from the Lord" (Proverbs 18:22, KJV). What does that mean to the ladies in the world? You don't have to look for a man; you are the treasure to be found. Just because you may be alone now does not mean it is forever. Sure, it doesn't feel good right now because of your natural and spiritual needs, but don't lower your defenses or your standards of what you prayed to the Lord for in what you desire your companion to be according to God's will. Be in fellowship with the Lord so when the right one does come looking for you, you don't miss the blessing of what God has in store for you.

A lot of people don't realize that if you take the step before the Lord in things that he has not prepared for you, you could be putting yourself in an unsafe predicament and a hellish life due to not waiting on the promise, taking on something that God has not prepared for you. Many make the mistake of trying to make something fit the mold when it hasn't been designed to. Women and men around the world have to realize and have faith that once you pray that very fervent prayer, it is settled with the Lord and you should not get in the way of the prayer waiting to be answered by God our Father.

Well, I know you must be wondering, whom are we talking about? We are talking about an all-American woman named Rebecca Washington. Like most women in the world, her self-esteem is low, which causes her to be very easily enticed by slick and sly men that she has encountered and taken on, allowing herself to get tangled up in awful and horrible relationships because of her fear of being alone. Rebecca works hard and has pretty much everything she needs in life, except for her ideal man. In her late twenties, she continues to go on the hunt for the man of her dreams, trying and allowing everything she can take until it has left her with scars, scars she has to learn to live with until true healing and restoration comes.

Will Rebecca, through her journey of finding the perfect man, lead her into a path of self-discovery of her own issues in her life that need to be addressed in order for her to be a whole woman instead of half of a woman. Will a complete healing and restoration take place, to be healed of life's scars and brought to a right relationship with the Lord and the man she has been waiting for all of her life?

one

An early July summer morning starts still and silent in Collierville, Tennessee, where Rebecca lies in bed in her elegantly decorated home. The rays of sunshine begin to peek through her curtains and custom-made blinds of wood mahogany, triggering her to wake up from her slumber. She begins to open her cherry brown eyes with a smile on her face from having another dream of finding the quote unquote right man made just for her. This is the daily struggle within her mind, even before she rolls out of bed. While lying with her arms stretched out, Rebecca turns her head and looks at the clock positioned on the nightstand: six o'clock.

Each day is filled with an earnest expectation of hope as she thinks, *This might be the day, the day that I meet my prince charming. Maybe on the job or on the way to the hospital for work. Who knows?* With slippers and robe at the end of the cherry wood canopy bed, wrapped in satin, navy blue sheets with an overstuffed down comforter on top rolled down neatly to the middle of the bed. She dismounts from the bed and goes to her bathroom with finely arrayed wallpaper and art, along with brushed nickel fixings around the bathroom. She goes into the bathroom to begin her daily beauty routine, which is not a hard task for her to accomplish. Due to her low self-esteem, she doesn't realize she has much natural beauty on the outside and in. But before she begins the routine, she stands there looking in the mirror, bent over with her arms spread slightly over the long granite sink vanity. She frowns at herself and thinks, *Who in the world are you, and what purpose do you serve? What makes you think that you can have the man of your dreams if you wait and be patient?* Then the other side of her conscience debates and says, *Girl, you know what you need to do. Get out there and do your own thing. No man is going fall in your lap. You have to get out there and look.*

She then straightens her posture up and turns to the side looks at her shape in the mirror, looking for flaws. Finishing her examination, she raises her hand up to the back of her head and lets her long raven locks of hair streaked with a few honey highlights throughout out her hair down out of the bun that it has been up in. Slowly walking over to her tub, she turns the knob and starts to run her bathwater. The phone rings.

"Who in the world could that be this early in the morning?" she said, walking over to pick the phone up in the bathroom. "Hello?" she answers with a hint of attitude.

"What's up, baby?" a male voice speaks.

She pauses. Then she says, "Who is this? And how may I help you this morning?" in her professional voice.

"You don't know who this is, baby girl?" the male voice says. "I can't believe that you've forgotten your man that quick, have you?"

Then she catches on to the voice after listening intensely. She says, "Jacob?"

He says, "Yeah, you don't know your man anymore?"

Leaning up against the marble tiled tub and kind of smiling in relief, she comments, "Oh, you're my man now?" With a slight pause after her question she says, "I haven't heard from you in over two and half weeks. You said that you really didn't want to be bothered with me the last time we spoke."

She places the phone on speaker then begins to brush her hair while walking back to the mirror, twirling her hair into a wild bun, securing it in place with hair clip for her bath.

Jacob speaks in his suave slick voice. "Aw, Cherie, you know that I didn't mean it; you know I can't live without seeing you."

Rebecca replies, "That's funny. If that were the case, Jacob, I would have heard from you in the past two weeks, at least once or twice."

Jacob slyly replies, saying, "You know me. I had business that I had to take care of, baby. You know I would have called you if I wasn't busy. I haven't been here; I've been out of town on business. Baby, you know how it is."

She quickly replies, "You do have a cell phone, right? You could have used it."

Jacob, still confident says, "I don't know why you're trying to give me a hard time because I know you want to see me. You know you still my girl."

She laughs letting the silence lengthen. She walks over and turns off the bath water.

Jacob, breaking the silence, says, "So am I going to see you later on today?"

She replies, "Um … I don't know. My schedule is probably going to be a little hectic today."

There is no reply from Jacob for a few seconds. Rebecca thinks really hard and looks at the time.

He says, "So you're not going to make an effort to see me today?"

She stares at the phone, worried that he might not be interested anymore. The silence in the room makes the clock's ticking seem louder.

"I will make time for you, even if I have to rearrange my schedule," she says shakily.

He replies, "All right, that's my girl. Meet me for dinner at our favorite restaurant around eight thirty p.m. and be dressed to impress."

Rebecca hears him hang the phone up before she can say bye. She looks at the phone receiver in unbelief of Jacob's action. She gets past that because that is what she has come to expect from him anyway. The conversation has taken up some time; it is now around 6:35 a.m. She quickly takes off her robe and nightclothes and steps into her Jacuzzi tub filled with bubbles. Sitting in the hot, steamy water, smelling of lavender, with her music playing the in the background, Rebecca slides down, lays her head back, closes her eyes, and thinks, *You are so gullible. I don't know why you agreed to meet with him; you know how he is and what he is about. All he wants to do is use you. He doesn't have your best interests at heart. He has played you in the past and hurt you emotionally, so why do you keep seeing him? What is this strange hold that he has over me?* She knows the answer to the question. It's because she just doesn't want to be alone, wanting someone to hold her and comfort her, desiring that companionship.

Finishing up her bath, she gets out of the tub and finishes dressing to depart for work, but before she leaves she has to straighten the house a little bit. She is compulsive with her cleaning; everything has to be in order and in its proper place. While walking to the door from the back of the house, which almost seems endless from where her bedroom is, she is decked out in a crisp nurse's uniform and hospital staff jacket with her purse and bag in hand. As she reaches the foyer area where the keys are sitting on the table, she thinks, *Man, I forgot my dress so I can meet with Jacob tonight. You shouldn't go anyway.* The battle continues within her conscience and flesh, but nevertheless, her constant need for companionship prevails, so she shuffles quickly back to the room to get the black dress and shoes, along with her decorative hair chopsticks. Finally proceeding to the door leading to the garage, ensuring nothing has been left out of place, she sets the alarm to the house and goes to her vehicle in the garage.

Opening the back passenger door of the Lexus RX 430, she places the items tenderly on the backseat, then gets in and starts up the truck, making sure her doors are locked as the garage lifts up. While pulling out of the garage, her cell phone rings.

Not really wanting to pick it up, she looks at the caller ID, and sees that it is her mother. Giving the command to answer the call through Bluetooth controls, the phone picks up.

"Good morning, Momma. What is it? I am on my way to work. Did you need anything?" she says.

"No, baby, I just wanted to check on you this morning to see how you were doing. I was thinking about you and just praying that God would keep you in his hand," Mother Washington says over the phone.

Rebecca rolls her eyes in the back of her head as she is driving out of her driveway because of her mother's reference to the Lord, thinking back to when she was a child of how they did nothing else but go to church.

"That's all you called to say, Momma? You didn't need anything?" she asked quickly.

"Well, I was calling to let you know that we are having revival services going on at the church this week and wanted to invite you out so you could hear a word from the Lord that might change your life. You never know; there may be man there for you too."

Rebecca shakes her head in disgust and unbelief. Since she has grown up and moved out of her parents' house, she has rarely gone to church.

"Becca?" Mom Washington says.

"Yes, ma'am, I'm here. I can't make it tonight, but I will try to make it tomorrow after I get off work, just because you asked," Rebecca says, looking at the time.

"Thank you, sweetie. You know, most of all, your father will be happy to see you as well," Mother Washington says quickly.

"Yes, I know. I'll do my best to be there," she answers, sighing at her mother's comments, knowing that her father will be contacting her soon.

Mother Washington says, "All right, honey. You have a blessed day. I'll be praying that your day is filled with God's favor."

"Thank you, Momma. Bye-bye," she responds as she hangs up.

With the call ended, her mind starts working overtime. *I don't know why you said you would be there at church knowing you really don't want to go. But I don't want to disappoint Mom and Dad as I always do.* Rebecca continues to reflect on growing up in the church and the things she did to rebel as a preacher's kid. Not that she was a bad child, but she was confused, always wondering why they were in church so much. With her parents' attention focused on the church, Rebecca felt no attention or interaction was there for her, which fostered feelings of abandonment in mind and spirit, which has somewhat brought her to the point where she is in life, looking for a companion.

Making up the time by increasing her speed, the drive isn't long to the hospital. Rebecca pulls into the hospital parking lot, turning off the music in the truck and putting on her game face for the workday. Turning the truck off, she reaches up and pulls the sun visor down to look at herself again in the mirror. She puckers up her lips, putting on lip liner along with lip gloss.

"Well, here goes another day; hopefully it's a good one," she says, putting her cosmetics back in her bag.

Before getting out of the vehicle, she scans the parking lot. Seeing no one in sight, she lets out an exhale. Opening the door, she gets out of the truck, walking at a quick pace to the hospital lobby doors with her purse and bag draping her shoulder, looking down at her delicately manicured hands and very low, sculpted fingernails. Still at a quick pace, she mentally begins preparing for the day that lies ahead in the hospital, knowing that challenges face her from every corner. She feels that as a woman she has to work twice as hard as men.

Once she's entered the hospital, she makes her way to the elevator, gliding through the hospital lobby with rapid steps, the picture-perfect woman on the outside with style, professionalism, and grace. As she passes people she knows through the lobby, a lot of them speak to her without hesitation because they know her personality and her work reputation. Being a young woman in the South has not always been easy, but she has continued to work hard, and it has paid off for her. Becoming one of the top nurses not just in the labor and delivery unit but in the entire hospital, Rebecca has encountered a lot of haters on her path in medicine and service to others, but she has not let that stop her hunger for success. *Boy, only if I could be this confident when it comes to being real and having a serious relationship with you, Lord, and even with men,* she ponders. Entering the elevator preoccupied, she takes a quick glance while the elevator doors are still open. Seeing no one in sight coming to the elevator, she closes her eyes and drops her bag on the floor and holds her purse in the crevice of her arm. Then she takes a deep breath in meditation for a moment, breathing in and out, slowing her heart rate down, listening to the calming instrumental music playing in the elevator.

While her eyes are closed, another passenger has entered the elevator as well and watches her. Feeling that she is not alone, she opens her eyes, focusing on the figure in green surgical scrubs.

"Well, hello there," he says.

She gathers herself, embarrassed that she has been caught with her eyes closed.

"Hello. It's Dr. Lowe, right? I didn't know you were in here," she says, her voice shaky.

"Dr Lowe, is it?" he says with his eyebrow raised. "You know me a little bit better than that, don't you? I thought we had moved to a first-name basis." With a smirk on his face, he says, "Trying to steal a few minutes for yourself before the workday starts?"

Feeling a little confused, trying to process and remember why he would mention that they should be on a first-name basis, Rebecca looks him up and down.

Dr. Lowe asks, "You don't remember me? My feelings are hurt; I am crushed."

He places his hand over his heart, slightly bending over with a playful frown on his face. "We sat down for lunch once before in the cafeteria a few months back. My name is Craig. Don't forget it this time," he says with a flirtatious smile.

"Oh ... okay. I am sorry; I really don't remember, but please forgive me. I have so many other things going through my mind right now. I probably wouldn't even remember my own child's name if I had one," she says.

They both laugh, and the elevator bell rings as Dr. Lowe's floor comes up and the doors part.

He says, "Well, it was really nice to see you again, Rebecca. Don't be a stranger. We ought to get together again for lunch sometime."

"I look forward to it," she says, smiling.

Then the elevator door shuts, continuing on to her floor while she thinks, *Could that have been the one?* She shakes her head and laughs, *No, it couldn't be.*

Looking at herself through the reflection on the shiny surface of the elevator doors, she takes her hands and uses them to rub her slicked-down hair back, making sure that everything is in place before she steps off the elevator heading to the labor and delivery unit. She takes just a few more deep breaths; the elevator bell rings, and the doors open to her unit. She picks up her bag and then exits the elevator, going around the round greeting desk where the nurses are sitting.

"Good morning, ladies," she says.

All the nurses look at her, returning her greeting. She keeps walking through the hallway of labor and delivery leading to locker/break room. Making it to the locker room, she opens up the door and enters, placing her purse on the desk off to the side and her bag in a storage cabinet. She takes a seat, letting out a sigh, glancing at few records in her in box that needed some signatures and finalizing for submission and closing out. Sitting back in the chair, she looks down at her nails and puts her hands out, looking at her bare ring finger.

Finally, the moment of silence is broken by her friend Grace knocking on the door as she opens it.

"Hey, Becky. What's going on this morning, girl?" Grace says as she takes a seat in front of the desk that Rebecca is sitting at and crosses her legs.

"Well, except for my mind being everywhere, I am here right now"—Rebecca twists the chair to each side with her head back—"trying to prepare myself mentally for this date tonight."

This immediately catches Grace's attention. "You have a date, Becky? Who is it with? I hope it is one of these fine available doctors in this hospital with no baggage and whorish intentions."

With Grace's right eyebrow raised and a smile on her face, Rebecca holds her head down, ashamed of the answer that is getting ready to part her lips. There is a pause of silence. Grace says, "Well?"

"It's Jacob," she says in a low voice.

"No! No! Becky, you know how things went the last time you paired up with him. He made it seem like he was a gentleman, but he has nothing but playing the little 'Mac Daddy' game on the inside, playing with your heart, and, girl, you are better than that."

Rebecca looks at Grace and hears her, but down in her heart, she is a slave to her desire and can't break the cycle that has started in life even though she wants to. The fear of being alone continues to drive her into bad decision-making.

Rebecca says, "I'm a big girl, sis. I can take care of myself. I know how he is. He isn't all that bad, but you know people can change."

Rising up from her seat, Grace stands there with her hand on her hip and a look of disappointment. "You know sometimes instead of waiting on somebody to change, you have to change yourself and move on into the next phase of your life. Hear me, Becky. You know I've got your best interests at heart," she says.

"I know you do. I know you always do; that's why I thank God I have you as my friend."

"All right, girl," Grace says with a motherly tone. Grace turns to exit the break room. "Well, I will see you later," she says as she walks out the door.

Rebecca turns around in the chair and looks at the personal shelves she has created filled with books of medical knowledge and instruction. Looking at these things, dealing with research and pictures of medical diagrams she has collected throughout the years in her little cubby space, even some books on being an OB/GYN, takes her into another thought.

She leans back in the small leather chair again and looks out the huge, double-layered glass window, being up on the eighth floor. She looks out at the sky and the atmosphere and closes her eyes again for another moment of meditation. Suddenly one of the nurses under her charge rushes in.

She says very quickly, "Rebecca, we need you in room 342. Mrs. Jones is complaining of piercing pain in her abdomen. She says it doesn't feel like contractions to her, along with the pressure at the bottom. We need you to come quick."

Popping up from the chair, Rebecca runs down the hallway holding on to her stethoscope, arriving at the room to hear Mrs. Jones screaming in pain. Two other nurses are already in the room trying to calm Mrs. Jones down. Rebecca quickly makes eye contact with Mrs. Jones.

"Okay, sweetie, I need you to do me a favor. Okay?" Rebecca says with her hand on Mrs. Jones's knee.

"What?" says Mrs. Jones loudly with her eyes bloodshot and widely opened.

"I need you to calm down for me, sweetie, to help relax your muscles so we can get some oxygen flowing for you and the baby. Okay?" she says, bringing a calm to the labor room.

"It's hard. I can't. It hurts so bad; it feels like someone is stabbing me."

Rebecca looks over to Nurse Stacy and asks, "What was she last when you guys checked her?"

"I checked ten minutes ago, and she was at eight," says one of the nurses.

Rebecca sits down at the edge of the hospital bed and asks her to lie back for her, and she slides the sheets up and puts a glove on to check dilation.

She tells Mrs. Jones, "I know this is going to hurt, honey, but I need to check you."

Rebecca checks her as the other nurses stand by, observing her style of working with the patients and their dilemmas.

"Yes, you're fully dilated, Mrs. J., and one hundred percent effaced. I don't want you to panic, okay? But the baby needs to be turned; it's coming out breech, which means the feet are coming first instead of the head. I need someone to contact Dr. Nobles and tell him he needs to make his way to labor and delivery, room 342 stat, possible emergency cesarean."

Rebecca tries to console Mrs. Jones. Sympathizing with her pain, she continues to talk her through, keeping her mind focused on the end result of her delivery. Swift and accurate decisions are made to bring the patient comfort quickly in order to bring the baby into the right position to be delivered.

Rebecca said confidently to the couple, "Seems this baby is trying to rush to make an entry here. I am going to attempt to turn the baby for you so you can deliver naturally since I know that's what you're trying to achieve.

"If this doesn't work, we have to do what's best for you and the baby, and that would be a C-section," Rebecca explains, sitting on the edge of the bed.

Looking in to Rebecca's eyes, Mrs. Jones trusts her completely, knowing she has the family's interest at heart. The nurses put an oxygen mask on Mrs. Jones and try turning the baby. The husband is on the side with a look of worry, and Stacy, one of the nurses from the ward, goes over to him and tries to reassure him that everything is going to be fine.

"All right, ladies. How are things coming?" Dr. Nobles says, clapping his hands together.

After looking at the progress of the baby on the contraction- and heart-monitoring machine, he looks at the couple.

"Everything looks good; the baby is responding well now, I see."

"What's her progress, Nurse Washington?" Dr. Nobles asks.

"Well, Doctor, the baby was coming out breech position, so we tried turning the baby in the right way. She is one hundred percent effaced and is ready to push if the baby has turned with the technique we used."

Dr. Nobles said with a surprised look on his face, "Rebecca, let me take a look-see. How are you holding up, Mrs. Jones?"

Sitting on the side of the bed, Dr. Nobles checks her progress, then looks up at Rebecca and then the Jones couple.

"Well, looks like we have success, ladies and gentlemen. All we have to do is start pushing, and we should have us a baby in a matter of moments," he says in a calm voice.

Sighs of relief come over the birthing room as all the nurses look at one another with a smile and look up to the ceiling, giving reverence to God. Thirty minutes pass, and the child born to the couple is a healthy son. They thank Rebecca and her nursing team for their concern, compassion, and diligence.

The hours pass, seeming to drag by, and the shift is now over. Rebecca finds her way back to the locker room and gets dressed for dinner. Most of the nursing staff has switched for the night, but one of her nurses pops by the locker room as she stands by the window peering out, looking at the night with her arms folded.

"Rebecca," the voice calls.

Rebecca turns around to make eye contact.

Stacy says, "I was very impressed by how you worked with us today. It feels really good working as a team. You know, you should think about actually becoming a doctor. I know that it sounds crazy coming from a fellow nurse—you know how we stick together—but your work is really impressive."

A smile comes across her caramel face as she replies, "Thank you so much. I really appreciate that; I really do."

Stacy smiles and tells Rebecca good night, leaving from the doorway. Rebecca returns to peering out the window; the lights are off with just a desk light on and light from outside. The streets of the city are not busy, going into deep thought of what this night may bring. Will it bring joy, or will it bring pain, which she is willing to risk trying to find a man? A good man at that. But hearing the ringing words that have been spoken to her once before: Just because they have great jobs doesn't always mean that they are good men. But the way she feels, she guesses it is a risk worth taking. *I don't want to be alone* is the thought that haunts her dreams, as she fears one day waking up old and childless, with no one beside her who loves her for who she is. Raising her arm to check the time on her watch, she rubs her arms *I guess it is time to go.* She turns to exit the locker room, picking up her purse and bag, before pausing at her storage cabinet to check her appearance in the long mirror, seeing how her black dress is fitting on her frame. With her soft and beautiful facial features and her hair cascading down her back, she is well beyond beautiful with grace and class, but her self-confidence says that she could look a little bit better and should lose some weight as well. Finally, she finishes her once-over and leaves for her date.

two

While driving through the traffic of Memphis heading downtown, Rebecca leans against the armrest of her truck, playing some slow R&B music on the radio and trying to get in a relaxed mood, praying repeatedly, *Let this be a good date. Please let this be a good date.* The vehicle comes to a red light. Stopping at the stoplight, she hears the phone ring and looks and sees that it is her dad.

"Hello, Father," she says, answering the cell phone.

"Hey! How is my princess doing?" he speaks in his deep raspy voice.

"I am doing fine, Daddy," she says while pulling off from the stoplight and continuing to drive.

He asks, "How was your day today?"

"It was busy and intense but all right," she says with an exhale.

"You know I have to call and check on my princess, right?"

"Yes, I know, Daddy."

"Are you coming to church tonight? I believe it is

going to be a time in the Lord," Father Washington says excitedly .

"No, Daddy. I am not going to be able to make it tonight; I have a prior engagement."

Being insightful as he always has been, he comments, "That means a date, right?"

"Yes, Father."

"All right. I am going to let you go now. I just wanted to check on you, that's all. I am getting ready to go into the church. I'll talk to you later, baby girl."

"All right, Daddy. Love you."

"Love you too, princess," he says, ending the conversation.

Hanging up the phone shortly, she arrives at the historic and legendary Peabody Hotel located on Union Ave at one of the prominent restaurant's within the Peabody establishment, the Chez Philip. She pulls up to where the valet service is. They open her door for her and help her out of the truck. "Good evening, ma'am," the valet says, giving her a number. She thanks him and puts a tip in his hand.

With her purse clutched close, she makes her way up the stair entrance of the restaurant, walking up to the hostess.

"Good evening, ma'am," the hostess says politely.

"Good evening," Rebecca says in return.

"What party are you dining with tonight?"

"Richards."

The hostess beckons for her to follow her to the specified reserved seating area. Following the hostess, she passes the coat checkpoint area through the glass doors into the restaurant, which is accented with crown moldings, luxurious pillars, and crystal chandlers, marvelous tapestries, and draperies. The soft lighting throughout the restaurant has set a mood for romance. The pianist plays a soft melody of jazz.

Rebecca scans the room in hopes that Jacob will already be there waiting on her, showing a sign that he is serious this time. She reaches the reserved table to find Jacob has not yet arrived. The hostess seats her at the table.

"Here you go, ma'am," the hostess said, giving her the wine menu.

"Thank you," she replies as she takes her seat, placing her purse on the table and placing some of her hair behind her ear.

A waiter comes up quickly, asking her if she will be dining alone or will someone be joining her, also inquiring if there is anything that she would like to drink.

"Just water for right now."

Troubled slightly that he is not there already, she feels that the date already has a bad start. She checks the cell phone to see if she missed any calls or text messages. After five minutes, she checks it again. Twenty-five minutes pass, and finally he shows up.

Jacob says, "Hey, baby. You look beautiful tonight." Unbuttoning his suit coat and placing his cell phone on the table, he takes a seat at the table across from her.

"Thanks," she says quickly.

"Is something wrong?"

"I should think so. Don't you, Jacob? I have been

here nearly thirty minutes, and you don't call or anything to let me know you're going to be late. From the way you called me earlier, I thought that you were going to be here waiting on me."

"I came, didn't I? I told you that I wanted to see you, right? I was busy; I got held up taking care of some business," Jacob said, gesturing with his hands. "Now, can we order so we can eat and enjoy one another's company, or are we going to fight and act childish?"

She wants to react to his demeaning answer, but instead, her heart gets in the way of the fact that he might get up and walk out on her and make her feel rejected.

Jacob says, "Come on, baby. You know me. Let's have a good time, okay? I know that you probably had a busy day at the hospital too. I had very busy day at my office. Let's just relax and be with each other. Now, come on. Give me that smile that can melt any heart."

Bringing her head halfway up, she smiles a little bit, entertaining Jacob's sly talk. After they talk, getting their little disagreement out of the way, they start into their dining experience. After an hour passes into the date, his phone rings, and he picks it up, glancing at the contact shown, then puts it back down with a suspicious and guilty look.

"Is something wrong?" Rebecca asks.

"No, of course not. What would make you ask that question?"

Folding her arms together she says, "Well, you looked at your phone like you wanted to answer, but you gave a look like you couldn't believe they were calling you right now."

"What? What you are talking about, Rebecca?" he said in a high-pitched voice. "Maybe I just wanted to spend time with you with no interruptions from anyone; maybe that is what it was, you think."

"Well, you could be right," she says, shrugging her shoulders.

Of course, ten minutes later, Jacob's phone rings again. Rebecca sighs and exhales, frustrated with the constant interruption. Then Jacob picks up the phone and greets whoever is on the phone and puts his index finger up to her and begins to speak really softly. Rebecca tries to listen to what he is talking about while he is turned to the side with his head down. Suspicious that it is another woman on the line with him, she folds her arms, staring at him to get off the phone. He glances at the displeasure on her face and puts his finger back up and then gets up from the table and goes toward the phone area of the restaurant. A look of unbelief comes over her round face, and she turns her head, staying in spite of her frustration.

"I am sorry, baby. I had to take that call. You know how business is," he says, returning to his seat.

Rebecca smartly replies, "Looked more like pleasure than business, Jacob."

"Now, why would you say that?" he says in his calm playboy tone. "You know I wouldn't disrespect you like that, no matter how I was in the past. This dinner was supposed to let you know that I have changed, girl."

He continues on his mission to convince her. She

looks up to the ceiling for a few seconds thinking, *Should I believe him? He seems so sincere, but I know how it has been in the past with him. But if I don't give him another chance, I would be going against what I told Grace, that people can change."* After all that has transpired so far, Rebecca talks herself into staying through dinner and the rest of the evening with Jacob. Instead of leaving, she renders him a smile that's inviting. He nods his head like, "Yeah that's it." He knows he has her wrapped around his finger.

Despite how the evening started, Rebecca enjoys his company. After dinner they go dancing, and now the evening begins to come to a close. They are on their way out to their cars. She looks at him, holding his hand, and then leans in and gives him a kiss on his cheek, telling him what a good time she had with him and thanks him. When she goes to let his hand go and go to her truck, he is still holding her hand. She looks at him as if to ask, "Are you going to let my hand go?"

"Is that it, baby?" he asks, looking at her with one raised eyebrow. "I know you have more for your boy, right?"

Feeling nervous of what he may want, she asks, "More like what, Jacob?"

"Hold on, baby. I'm not talking about a one-night stand, if that is what you think," he says, stepping back a little with his arms bent and slightly lifted. "I just want a little kiss and hug you know. You know me, and we've been on few dates. We do have a history together."

"That's the problem; we have history," Rebecca says, lifting her necklace away from her neck.

"All I want is little kiss on the lips. Evidently you don't trust yourself," he says.

Taking the challenge of his manipulation, she grabs him by the lapels of his suit and pulls him and kisses him softly. Jacob puts his hands around her waist and holds her close to him. They fall up against the truck, and the kiss breaks.

In her mind Rebecca thinks, *Oh my God. What did I just do?* Looking at him, she tells herself, *All right. I need to say good night and get home.*

"Thank you. Now that's what I was talking about," he says, putting her into her truck.

She wants to ask him to come with her, but she keeps her mouth closed. He walks to his car and drives off. Bumping her head gently up against the leather steering wheel she thinks, *Oh my God. Why did you let him leave? You know you wanted more than that!* Turning the key quickly to start up the truck, she drives off. The ride home seemed like a long one, as she thinks of what she should have done so he wouldn't go. Finally, she arrives home, pulling into the garage, making sure everything around her is secure. The garage door rolls down, and she gets out of the truck, getting the rest of her belongings, and walks into the house. Once in the house, she starts getting everything situated for the next day, checking her messages on the answering machine and walking to the foyer area to put her keys in a bowl on the table. The doorbell rings. Slowly walking to the door, scratching her head in confusion,

Rebecca thinks, *Who is ringing the door and coming to my house at this late hour?* Going to the door with caution, peeking out the window, she sees that Jacob's sport Jag is sitting out there. She opens up the door, getting ready to ask him what he's doing there. Then he grabs her and kisses her passionately, but she resists him; he still continues to kiss her on her neck in the doorway. Eventually she gives in to him and her desire not to be alone, and he carries her to the bedroom.

Morning comes swiftly as the wind whistles and blows through the trees. Awakened suddenly by sound of the alarm clock on the nightstand, Rebecca finds herself turned on her side naked under the satin sheets. She turns to greet Jacob but finds he's gone from her bed and the house without so much as a good-bye. Sitting up on the bed with the sheets clasped to her chest, she brings her knees to her chest. Putting her arms around her knees, she lowers her head and begins to shake her head in regret. Turning to look at the clock showing eight o'clock and seeing the time is far spent for the morning, she picks up the remote to turn on the music throughout the house. Wrapping the sheet around her body, she walks slowly into the bathroom to turn on the shower water. She turns and looks in the mirror in disgust, but the war going on in her mind asks her, *Why are you disgusted with yourself, girl? You got exactly what you wanted. You knew you wanted him; that is what the whole date was about. You knew that he wasn't going to change and was no good. Just be honest with yourself; you really didn't want that commitment with him. You knew he would do exactly what you thought he would do.* Rebecca turns away from the mirror. *No that is not what I wanted or what I have been praying for. Lord, help me.*

While in the bathroom, she puts on her robe and comes back out into the room to open up the curtains to look out at her backyard, which gives her solace. After a few minutes, she walks back into the bathroom. Looking in the mirror again, she gets her brush and begins to brush her long locks while the shower water runs in the background, creating a lot of steam. Glancing at the clock in the bathroom to check the time, she keeps in mind the daily tasks that she has to complete on her day off work. Opening the shower door and stepping in, she puts her head up against the tile and begins to weep. Even though the night with Jacob gave her a moment of pleasure, she still feels low, like a trash receptacle. She fooled herself thinking that he was going to be there when she woke.

After her shower, Rebecca goes into the kitchen to make breakfast. She notices the light on the answering machine flashing. Rushing over to the machine, she pushes the button.

"Hey, Becky. This is Jacob. I am sorry that I left, but you know how it is. I had to take care of some business, and I also had to get in to work kind of early. Had some clients that I had to meet. I'll see you later on, all right? You my girl."

"Hello, sweetheart. It's Mom. I just wanted to see if we were still on for lunch. And I wanted to find out if you were still coming to church tonight. Love you. Bye-bye."

After listening to her mom's request, Rebecca calls her back, confirming their date. While in the kitchen still, she takes a seat at the breakfast table and looks out her window. In spite of certain events, she is grateful for all the things that she has acquired in her short lifespan, figuring, *A pastor's child that was raised in the church always goes back to some of their root training, giving God thanks for what he continues to do for us, in spite of our shortcomings.* While still seated at the table, she turns to look at the news on the TV above the countertop in the kitchen; she starts scanning the area around her to make sure that everything is clean and in order before she goes out for the day. A thought comes while she sits with her feet propped up in another chair: *Life could be easier if I wouldn't try to control everything and would just go with the flow sometimes.*

Later that morning, she rendezvous with her mom at the day spa for some mother-daughter time.

"Hey, Momma," Rebecca says as she pulls up.

Her mother turns around. "Good morning, baby. How are you this wonderful morning? I almost started without you. You see I am on my way inside already. I am trying to get my full service on today."

Rebecca laughs as she pulls into a parking space, quickly getting out with her sweat suit on and hair pulled into a ponytail.

"Don't you look all cute and laid back this morning," Mother Washington says as Rebecca walks up to her.

"I need to get a good massage because I am just a bundle of nerves."

"Do you want to talk about it?"

"No, not right now, Momma."

They both walk up the steps going into the day spa and are greeted by the receptionist. "Good morning, ladies. How are you doing this fine morning? Ready to be pampered? What's the name under the appointment today?"

Mother Washington speaks. "It's under Washington, dear. Thank you."

Not a moment later, the escorts come out to take them back to the dressing area.

Forty-five minutes later, they are in their robes and have had their manicures. Now they are having a foot massage done, along with a pedicure side by side. Rebecca looks at her mom then turns her head back and then glances at her mother again.

"Mom, I don't know what I am doing with my life," she says with her head down.

Mother Washington looks surprised by the statement made. She gains her composure, not having thought that her daughter would confide in her or ask her for any type of advice.

"Well, you know, I—"

"You know, Mom. I would really like it if you could just talk to me real, just mother and daughter, instead of putting the Lord in it. You know what I mean. I have heard that all my life growing up, living with you and Dad, even up until now. No disrespect intended. I just would like my mother for a minute or two, not Evangelist Washington."

Mrs. Washington is silent, taking a second to digest what her daughter has just requested of her.

"I know that when you guys were growing up, your father and I didn't spend the time with you that we should have. I know we always did a lot of ripping and running, doing things for the church instead of paying more attention to our children at home."

Rebecca is caught off guard. *I can't believe what I am hearing right now.*

Mother Washington continues to speak. "I know that my way of doing things probably really took a toll on you children, especially you. We should have dealt with you guys according to your different personalities, not catering, but trying to relate. So right now, right here, I want to apologize to you for not being there as I should have as your mother."

Rebecca looks astonished, thinking, *I must be dreaming. I can't believe all of this stuff that is coming out of my mother.* She has always known her mother to be a woman to make no apologies for how she ran her house and served the Lord and church.

"Momma, why are you saying all of this?" Rebecca said, still in shock at her mother's confession to her.

Mother Washington speaks, "Baby, I know that you're unsure of so many things in regards to the job. You probably want more, but I know that there is something that every woman wants more, even if she has success."

The pedicurists become quiet.

"It's the love of a good man. That's every single woman's prayer, to have someone to love and someone to love her for who she is. You've done all right in your life as far as what I can see, but I know you're having trouble with men; Mother knows what she's talking about. I had the same problem at one time, a weakness for fine men with good jobs."

Rebecca's mouth drops open in amazement.

"Yeah, I know it is hard to believe, because all you know is the saved church side. I didn't want my children to know that side of me for fear you would go down that same road. Instead of being honest with you all, I caused you to have trouble now. You have to get a grip on things before they get a grip on you and you get caught in a situation you don't want to be in. Especially giving yourself to them, being a receptacle of their spirit and craziness. The last thing you want is to end up with a belly full of problems that leaves you attached with a no-good man for the rest of your life. Thank God I was fortunate and the Lord spared me," Mother Washington says, lying back in the chair.

"Mom, how do you know all this about me?" Rebecca asks as she sits up.

Mother Washington reaches over to her, patting her hand. "Becca, baby, I know because I have been through it. Been there, done that. I know the regret of giving in to our unhealthy desires. Now you know, baby I have to take it to the spiritual aspect of things, because there is a natural side and spiritual side to things in life."

Rebecca sits back, looking down at the pedicurist working on her feet.

"Now, baby girl, the only way to be free of these things is to realize that things aren't in your control but the Lord's. Let these things go so they don't control your life. You understand?" Mother Washington says, still touching her hand.

"Yes, ma'am," Rebecca replies, nodding her head. "It's just so hard, Momma, to let go of some things when they feel so good to you, you know."

"This man has really gotten to you, but let me ask you this. Has he, even one time, told you that he loves you?" Mother Washington asks.

Rebecca quickly replies, "I have never asked for him to or implied such a thing because I didn't want to run him off."

"I am telling you, if he hasn't put forth the effort to show you that you are number one, that you matter in some type of way, why waste precious time in your life with him?"

"I know, but—" Rebecca says, trying to plead her case. Her mother cuts her off, interrupting her plea.

"There are no buts to this. Either he is or he isn't. Don't lower your standards and expectations, honey, just because you think you are not going to find someone when you want them."

"It's hard, especially when everyone else around you has someone and all you have is your job and home."

Mother Washington looks at Rebecca and puts her hand under her chin and lifts her head, looking at her.

"Just be patient, love. God sees, and he knows all about your problems, issues, and every situation that you face. Just relax and let him take control. You're a beautiful, successful young lady that has everything going for her. Just wait. What God has for you, it is for you."

Nodding in agreement, Rebecca sits back in the chair, still amazed, for she has never ever seen this side of her mother before, where she could relate and actually talk on her level. That experience with her mother reached down to her innermost being and repaired a few things that she felt had been broken in their relationship. Rebecca actually felt important today and loved by her mother, not neglected as she did in her childhood, feeling that many things were put before her. It was always church and not the family, but today it changed something in the very foundation of her mind, taking her down the road of repair and healing.

three

Later, in the early evening, it has become still, hot, and humid. No longer with her mother but still amazed at the day that she's had thus far, Rebecca goes and gets her hair done and decides to meet Grace for dinner. Coordinating with each other, they decide to meet up at J. Alexander's restaurant. Grace has already made it to the spot inside of the restaurant and is waiting on Rebecca. Walking from the car, on her way into the restaurant, she hears her name being called from across the parking lot. Suddenly, there is a slight breeze in the air blowing her elegant purple sundress in wind. Turning, she is surprised to see it is Dr. Craig Lowe.

"Dr. Lowe, I mean, Craig. It's nice to see you. What are you doing here?"

"I am meeting someone for dinner here. You?"

"Oh, I am meeting Grace for a little dinner before I go to church."

"May I escort you into the restaurant, lovely lady?" he says, putting his arm out for her.

Blushing, she says, "Thank you very much" as she takes his arm and walks toward the double doors.

Rebecca looks at him. "Your date probably won't appreciate some other woman hanging on her man for the night."

He looks at her and smiles. "I am pretty sure she is not here yet. It won't hurt to be polite to another beautiful lady."

As they enter Rebecca sees Grace sitting there with her fiancé, Darrell with a smirk on her face.

"Hey, girl," Grace responds, getting up to hug Rebecca.

While embracing her, Rebecca whispers, "Can I see you in the restroom for a second, please?"

Grace laughs and agrees. They turn to the gentleman and ask them to excuse them for a second.

They both enter into the ladies restroom, and Rebecca hits Grace on her arm, laughing. Grace bursts out laughing.

"I can't believe you. What have you done, Grace?" she says, holding on to Grace's arm.

"What? It's just a little dinner. It seems like you two were getting along quite well before you walked in," Grace says, still laughing softly.

"So this is supposed to be a double date, huh?" Rebecca says, looking in the mirror, putting on her lip liner, along with lip gloss.

"Well," Grace says with her hand on her hip, leaning up against the brown stone wall, still smiling.

"I can't believe this. Girl, you know I promised my

mother that I was going to church tonight," Rebecca says as she touches up her makeup.

"Becky, I couldn't help it, girl. He came to me and said that he wanted to meet with you again and didn't want to take the chance of you turning him down since you really didn't remember him when he got in the elevator," Grace says, explaining the circumstance.

"I do have to admit he is persistent. I just saw him but didn't really give him the time of day," Rebecca says.

Grace looks at her like she is crazy. "Why, girl? I can't believe that. The man is fine and seems very cultured and gentlemanlike."

"Well, I guess it was because I was still thinking about Jacob," Rebecca says, looking through her purse.

"Oh, Lord," Grace replies.

"What?" Rebecca whines.

"I am not going to even go into that conversation regarding that player. Are you almost done, Becky?" Grace says with one hand out and another on the door.

Rebecca looks at her and shakes her head. "If I would have known that I was going on a date, instead of just you and me, I would have been a little bit more prepared or ready."

"You don't need to do all that. A man sometimes needs to see your natural beauty.

"That's easy for you to say. You have a man. In fact, a man you're going to marry."

"Whatever. Let's not keep these men waiting," Grace says, dancing around a little.

Coming out of the ladies room, Grace and Rebecca see that the men are nowhere to be found. Searching the restaurant, they spot them by the windows. The guys wave at them. Rebecca and Grace look at each other. Grace says to her, "They've got nerve to leave us."

As the women walk over to the table, the men stand up, greet them, and help them into their chairs.

Rebecca comments as she sits, "We thought you guys had left us or something."

Craig quickly replies, placing his hand on her shoulder, "Why would we do that to two such beautiful women? The table became available, and we didn't want to lose it."

Rebecca looks at Dr. Lowe and grins. "Well, flattery will get you everywhere."

Grace and Darrell look at each other and laugh.

Rebecca says jokingly, "Well, Dr. Lowe, or I should say Craig, I guess I am your date for the evening."

"Well, you don't have to be jealous then of the beautiful lady I escorted into the place," he says in response.

They both laugh. Darrell looks at both of them and smiles.

"Well, I guess both of you are hitting it off pretty well," Darrell comments.

"Aw, man. It's just a little jokey joke we had before we came in," Craig says.

Grace looks impressed and satisfied by all that is going on with the date, but she is very watchful, looking out for her friend. The evening continues with success. Rebecca thinks things could be promising with this man, but she is skeptical, labeling all men the same. Looking at her watch she says, "Oh my god, guys. I have to go."

"Why?" Doctor Lowe says, looking disappointed.

"I told you. I have to go to church. I promised my parents I would come," Rebecca says while standing up, putting money on the table for her meal, but Dr. Lowe puts it back in her hand.

"It would be my pleasure to pay for this meal for you."

She looks at Grace and Darrell and then looks at him. "Well, thank you. That is really nice of you; I appreciate it," she says and then runs out.

Driving along the highway, Rebecca thinks of the evening with the doctor and what a success it was, feeling somewhat cheated that she had to leave early. But her promise to her mother and father comes to mind, and that is all she can think about right now. Arriving at the church, she pulls up in to the parking lot and has flashbacks of coming as a little girl, even a teenager with all the stuff she used to get into being a PK (preacher's kid). Getting out the truck and walking through the parking lot, she sees her older sister Paige with her belly all swollen from pregnancy and with her two children trailing behind her. Rebecca walks up to her and gives her a hug.

"Hey, big sis. How are you doing?" she says. She touches Paige's belly and then hugs her nephew and niece.

"Why are you so late, Rebecca?" Paige asks.

Rebecca wants to say, "None of your business," but

she gives an opposite reaction thinking of how Paige and she usually argue.

"Well, I had something come up at the last minute, but I am here now. Sweetie, how are you doing in this hot weather, carrying around those babies in that belly of yours?" Rebecca says.

"I could be doing better if I were sitting down instead of doing all this running around," Paige complains, carrying a tray of food.

"Where is Tyler?" Rebecca asks.

"In the church, in the pulpit. Where else would he be? Not out here helping me, that's for sure. I had to get the children ready, and I wasn't feeling too well myself, so it took me a little bit," Paige says.

"Well, sista, let me take that from you. I'll take it to the church fellowship hall and put it in the kitchen. Then I will bring Justin and Justine in with me when I get them situated. You go rest and sit down; I got them."

Paige, with a surprised look on her face, walks into the church building. "Are you sure about that?" she says, questioning the gesture of kindness.

"Yeah, sure, of course. This is nothing," Rebecca says.

Paige makes her way to the sanctuary down the long halls of the church.

Rebecca walks to the church fellowship hall with the twins, where more people are working in the kitchen. With her back turned so she can see the children following her, she opens the doors with her butt and back. She hears greetings from some of the church staff that she hasn't seen for a while.

"Hello, Becca. How are you doing this evening, darling?" says very familiar voice.

"Hello, Ms. Brooks. How are you doing?"

"I am blessed, baby, and highly favored of the Lord," Ms. Brooks responds.

"Here you go," she says as she hands the food over the fellowship window counter into the kitchen.

"You have the two little angels I see," Ms. Brooks says, smiling at the two-year-old twins.

"Yes, I figured I'd give Paige a little break and let her relax some," she says.

She gently pulls the twins to her, looking at them, checking them over, and giving them a little snack before they go into the church while sitting at the table in the fellowship hall, Rebecca lets the children run around for a few minutes in the oversized fellowship hall arrayed in dark brown curtains, hardwood floors, and contemporary fixings all around to make any person feel warm and at home. She gazes out of the window to the parking lot, escaping, planning, sketching, and trying to fit Jacob in. Thoughts invade her mind of the doctor, and she wonders if there might be potential there. She still wants to be in control. She feels trapped into the mind frame of traditions, of being married at a certain age and having kids. She looks at her sibling's life, then compares it to how empty her life seems. After thoughts of grandeur pass, she calls to the kids; they run to her, shouting her name. Calming them down, she takes them out of the fellowship hall so they can go into the sanctuary of the church.

She exits the fellowship hall, smiling and playing with the children as they walk the passageway of the church halls. Something catches her eye. In that very moment, she can't believe her eyes. They are focused and engaged on the figure walking up to her slowly. Her heart pounds within her chest, and her breathing picks up a little. The surroundings seem to slow down as she sees her love from her teen years, the one she thought she would marry, but it didn't work out that way. Things seemed to go sour after their long-committed relationship. *After so many years, here he is now, walking toward me.* Speechless, she stops in her tracks and stares. Philip continues to walk toward her and then embraces Rebecca with a tender hug.

"How you doing, girl? God, you look good," he says.

Rebecca is still without words; she continues to hold onto the twins' hands. "Yeah, you too. I can't believe it," she responds.

"You're really here," she says, still with an expression of shock.

Leaning up against the wall, he speaks. "I have been traveling and preaching. You know how it is, being in the church, always trying to make sure that we have some engagements. I really haven't had much time for anything else."

Still amazed at the fact he is standing there in front of her, Rebecca bends down to pick up Justin, who has started whining.

Philip looks her up and down. "You have to be married by now, right?" Philip inquires.

Rebecca smiles at his question, because she is still interested in him.

"No, I am not married yet; you know, the right one hasn't really asked me," she says, tilting her head to the side.

Philip stands there and folds his arms and puts his finger on his chin.

"Well, I need to get in this sanctuary with these babies. I don't want to miss the service. You know how it is," she says, holding Justin and taking Justine's hand.

"Yeah, yeah. I know how it is, but you got to let me holler at you later, all right? We have a lot to catch up on," he says.

Rebecca walks off, holding one baby in her arm and the other's hand, smiling and talking to them, keeping their energy under control.

In the church sanctuary, the service is high and full of energy with the spirit of the Lord in the place and praises and singing going forth. Rebecca finds a spot to sit in with the children. While they are playing and sitting on the floor with their toys, words of encouragement come from the pulpit in a very wise and uplifting way. The words catches her attention as she thinks of what she has heard the past couple of days.

"Women, you need to know who you are. God has made you special. There is no one else like you, mighty and virtuous women of God. You are to be pursued with honor and dignity. Stop lowering your standards; you are a jewel to be found and worthy of a good man that loves God and loves you as Christ loved the church, so much that he gave his life for the church," the preacher says.

Touched by the spirit and the words of encouragement coming forth, she begins to cry a little with her head down and then looks at the children playing intently with their toys between the church pews. An hour has passed, and the service is coming to a close. Feeling someone is watching her, she scans the church sanctuary and sees Philip watching her. Standing up at the other end of the pulpit behind the organ, he gestures to her to wait on him after church.

Families and church members exit the sanctuary. Still with the twins, Rebecca walks over to catch her dad, who is talking to a church member with her mother. Rebecca kisses her mother on the cheek and whispers to her while holding Justine, "Thank you so much, Mom, for what you told me earlier."

Mother Washington just nods in agreement to her.

Her father looks at her and says, "Hey, baby girl. I didn't see you in church earlier."

"Yes, Daddy, I was here," she says, getting ready to explain.

"That's because she was helping me, Daddy," Paige says as she comes over and interrupts.

"Oh, okay. I guess you're excused," Preacher Washington says, smiling and laughing.

Rebecca looks at him and laughs but kind of rolls her eyes off to the side so her father can't see. Preacher Washington looks at his other daughter, Paige, and touches her stomach and then looks at Rebecca.

"When are you going to give us one of these like your sister?"

Mother Washington looks and him and grabs his arm, shaking her head.

"You know, Philip is back in town now. I believe he will be staying around this time. You ought to get up with him, baby girl. He's a good man, if you catch my drift, comes from a good family," Father Washington says suggestively.

Paige and Rebecca shake their heads; then Rebecca tells her dad, "Yeah, Daddy. I know. I hear you." Then she walks off after giving Paige her children.

Preparing to get in to her truck, she is confronted by Philip running up to her.

"Bee! Bee! Where are you going? I told you to hold up, girl. I wanted to talk to you. Why are you rushin' off?"

Rebecca looks at him, sitting in the truck with the door open. "What do you want, Philip?" she says with an attitude.

"All right, Bee. What's up with all the hostility? I'm just trying to holler at you since we haven't seen each other in quite a while," he says.

"What? Do you figure that since you're back you can hook up with me and get you some booty like old times, huh?" she says.

"It's not even like that, Bee. I am different now."

"Please, boy, you haven't changed. I still see you as the same boy as when we were growing up. You dogged me when you didn't want to be with me anymore instead of just being honest with me. You really hurt me, Philip. I thought you and I had more than that," she says.

"That's what I was trying to talk to you about. I am sorry about all that stuff from the past. I was going to ask your forgiveness, but you seemed like you didn't really want to talk to me in church. I just figured I could catch you after church. Maybe we could get something to eat or talk, that's all," he says.

"Oh really," Rebecca says, holding on to the truck door.

"Yes, really. Come on, Bee. Please," he says.

Finally giving in, she takes her hand off the door and puts it on the steering wheel of the vehicle, with her head down. Philip kneels down by the door opening, looking up at her.

"Please, Bee. You can even drive; you don't have to ride with me. Just come with me so we can talk, that's all," he says, persuading her.

Half an hour passes as they sit in each other's company at International House of Pancakes in Germantown.

"Well, Bee," Philip says. "I know you're waiting on an explanation. I do apologize for the way things ended between us."

"I still don't understand why. Things seemed perfect for us," Rebecca comments.

"See, that is the thing. It seemed perfect, which doesn't excuse the way I treated you," Philip replies.

Quickly responding, she says, "I was ready to give everything for you, Philip. We had a plan for our lives together."

"That's the thing; we had a plan, but we really didn't seek God about it at the time. We were young.

Everyone in the church was pushing for us to be together, and to be honest, I was not ready for marriage and children. To tell you the truth, I wasn't ready to be a preacher. I was still doing things wrong, things God had to forgive me for," he says, placing his hand upon hers.

Rebecca begins to think. "What things?" she asks.

"That's between me and God. I'm not pulling up any past things. My main thing was to set things straight between you and me."

The waitress brings their food, and Philip looks at Rebecca's order. "Bee, you sure you are going to be able to finish all of that? I might have to eat some of that for you," he says, laughing.

"I am just a little bit more famished than what I am usually."

Philip starts to explain how things were going during high school, reassuring Rebecca that his leaving Tennessee had nothing to do with her.

In the church they grew up in, usually preachers' kids married others preachers' kids to ensure good stock. Philip felt like he had not finished being a kid yet. The saying goes usually the preacher's kids are the worst children in the church. Even though he and Rebecca had a relationship together, he was a player's player. Even after a two-hour conversation and a meal, nothing could take away the pain that Rebecca endured from the breakup of their relationship. Due to today's events, now she feels that she can move on, dealing with that chapter of her life, but there is an unexpected twist to all of this.

Rebecca says, "I appreciate your doing this, telling me now even though it's ten years later, but why now?"

"Because I realize now what I had then, how badly I messed up, and I was just wondering and hoping that there might be a chance that we might be able to see each other since I am back in town now, that is, if you don't have someone in your life already," he says, looking unsure.

"Well, I am kind of seeing somebody, but it's an on-and-off thing," Rebecca says.

He says, "You mean to tell me that this man hasn't locked down a beautiful sister like you? He must be a fool."

"You think I am beautiful?" she asks.

"Of course, Bee. You have always been beautiful; everybody knows that, at least I thought you knew that when we were together," he says.

There is an awkward pause between them.

Then Philip makes a suggestion to her. "Okay, Bee. This is what I purpose then: we see each other; I don't want to push hard, because I do know you are a woman worth waiting for."

The words he speaks begin to strike her attention, making an impression upon her that she is willing to see to fruition. She would have never expected to see her longtime love again. A love she thought had died a long time ago with his leaving town and her life has now resurfaced stronger than she ever could have imagined in the stage of her life right now. With Philip's request she agrees to begin their courtship again hoping this time it will be success. The funny thing is, life always throws you twists and turns, and with the life that Rebecca has become accustomed to, she really knows how to deal with them as they come.

Two months have passed. Rebecca and Philip continue their courtship with one another despite a few ups and downs. They can only see each other as Rebecca's busy schedule permits, which conflicts with his different business ventures and preaching. The season has now transitioned to the end of the summer, the early part of September, and Rebecca is in her usual place in the designated break/locker room at her desk. The shift and the day are going by kind of slowly and lazily since it is a hot and usually muggy day outside and just all around quiet. Who should so happen to drop by to see her, as she is so intently into her study and research on different items dealing with pregnancy, but Dr. Lowe speaks. "Hello, Rebecca. How are you doing today?"

"Oh my god. Hey, Craig. How are you? Haven't seen you in a couple days. How's everything been going?" Rebecca says.

"I had little time available for vacation. So I figured I'd go and get some R & R, you know. It's hard to get a break from the medical field when you're so in demand. I was wondering, if you weren't doing anything, would you want to go grab a quick bite to eat? You've been on my mind, so I figured I'd stop by and see you," he says.

Popping up immediately from her seat, she walks to him, "It's about time for me to take a break to eat anyway. Sure. I'd be glad to. Let me just inform the other nurses on staff that I am going to take a quick break to eat and where I will be," she says picking up the phone.

She makes the phone call informing the staff. They make their way to the cafeteria, leaving from the break room, engaging in conversation of their last encounter at J. Alexander's on the surprise date. They laugh and smile with one another in the elevator, and soon the ride is over, and the doors open. They just so happen to meet Philip as they are coming off of the elevator. Philip's face is distorted with displeasure as he spots Rebecca with another man. Craig looks at him and then starts to greet him, but Philip just turns to Rebecca, giving her eye contact only to talk, ignoring Craig. Dr. Lowe just looks at him, shrugging slightly, telling Rebecca he will meet her in the cafeteria when she is done.

Philip looks at Craig walking away and then looks at Rebecca and lifts his hand in gesture, pointing at the doctor as he is walking away.

"What's that all about?" he says.

"Are you serious? We were just getting ready to eat during the free time we have," Rebecca says.

"Well, I was coming to surprise you for lunch. I wasn't doing anything, but it looks like you have plans already," he says.

As he begins to walk away, she grabs his arm. "I don't know what your problem is and who this person I am talking to right now, but you show up to my job unannounced; I didn't know you were coming. I would have gladly sat down with you for lunch, but right now, I don't even want to look at you anymore until you get yourself together. Let me know when the Philip I know returns," she says, letting go of his arm.

Rebecca walks off to catch up to Dr. Lowe. Philip is left standing there. He walks through the revolving doors of the hospital and exits.

Another day has come to a close at the hospital, and Rebecca is at home now getting ready to eat. While sitting, she looks around the family room decorated in black, burgundy, and gold to see if anything needed to be changed. Seeing that she can find nothing to change, she turns her attention back to her meal and the television and relaxes. When she finishes dinner, she places her plate on the coffee table. Then a few minutes later, she feels a little funny and sits up, wondering if the feeling will pass. After a few minutes more, the feeling seems to settle a little. She lies back down, and then all of sudden she leaps up and runs to the hallway bathroom and throws up. Sitting on the rug by the toilet, she gathers her strength and stands up by the sink and runs some cold water through her hands and splashes her face with the water and wets a rag to pat her face and neck. Looking around curiously, she thinks, *I must have eaten too much today. The heat and humidity must have soured my stomach.* She walks back to the family room, picking up her plate taking it over to the kitchen with granite black countertops. While she is rinsing off the dishes and placing them in the dishwasher, the doorbell rings. She turns around and looks at the clock on the wall. *Who in the world could that be at this hour?*

She walks slowly to the door, continuing through the foyer accented with dark brown travertine tile. Being cautious, she then looks through the peep hole of the big door, then looks through the bunched curtains of the side window to see if she can see a car. The person's face is covered by two dozen roses. Figuring this could only be one person showing up at this hour, she swings the door open.

"I don't know why you are here after—"

The roses drop from the face of the individual. "Philip," she says, surprised.

"You were expecting someone else?" he says, smiling to her surprise.

"What are you doing here?" Rebecca says, holding the door.

"Well, I figured I owed you an apology for what happened earlier today at the hospital," he responds, holding the roses out to her.

Caught off guard, she asks him, "How did you know where I live?"

"I called and asked your father. What's with the third degree? Can a brother get invited in?" he says as he hands her the roses.

Opening the door more, she invites him in. Coming into the home, he looks around.

"Man, girl, this house is bad. How are you paying for this?" he comments.

She turns around and looks at him as she walks down the hallway to the kitchen. With her head tilted to the side, she replies, "It's not hard, especially with the advice and guidance I got in investments and help from my father along with my job as a nurse."

"Man, you are really doing your thang, girl. I wish I had half the place like this," he says.

Walking out the kitchen across the hall to her pantry closet, she gets some vases for the flowers and comes back into the kitchen, asking him, "Philip, you mean to tell me that you don't even have a place to stay?"

"Oh yeah, of course, Bee. You know me. I always got something going on to take care of myself. I have a little real estate, but it's not here in Tennessee," he says.

While putting the water in the vase, Philip comes from around the bar portion of the counter of the kitchen overlooking the sink around behind Rebecca while she is talking, looking over her shoulder. Rebecca leans forward, asking him what is he doing. She turns around, and he puts his hand on her shoulders, letting them slide down to sides of her arms.

"What are you doing, Philip?"

"I am apologizing," he says.

"I thought you already did.," she says, breaking his hold on her arms and walking over behind the island in the kitchen. Looking at him with concern, she says, "Philip, what exactly did you think was going to happen when you came over tonight again unannounced?" Still keeping eye contact with him, she leans forward on the island.

"I am sorry, Bee. Just looking at you, I kind of lost myself for a moment. I just wanted to sit and chill with you and talk of old times, that's all," he says, beckoning to her.

"That's all, huh?" she questions him, unsure of his motives.

"Yeah, that's all."

With his request to sit for a while and talk of the past, the old times bring some joy to Rebecca and a little pain, but she continues to conjure up feelings of old for Philip. Starting to look at him in that old way that she used to, she places her hand on his shoulder tenderly. They sit on the sectional with her feet off the floor and tucked under her skirt. They share laughs of past events between each other, and he looks at her and then leans in and kisses her.

"What are you doing?" she asks. "You can't do this. You're a preacher, Philip."

"I know, but you are my one temptation," he replies and kisses her again.

Rebecca comments quickly, "I can't let you do that to yourself."

"Bee, I am still in love with you, girl," he says, holding on to her.

A look of complete and utter awe comes over her face. Before she knows it, the feelings of old take her over, and she gives in to him totally, locking him in an embrace and pulling his shirt off. They give in and then take it to the bedroom. In her mind she can't believe what she is doing after just trying to make a change, but the other side of her tells her that this is what she has been waiting for. She falls asleep on his chest after the moment of lust and passion has been fulfilled.

Morning light breaks through the house like an

explosion as the sun rises, coming through the blinds and curtains. Rebecca's eyes open to the light in her bedroom before the alarm goes off; she rises up, looking hung over from last night's escapades. Suddenly, while she is sitting in bed, she gets this overwhelming feeling of nausea and dizziness. Lying back on the bed, she thinks that it will pass, but then it comes again. Her eyes begin to get watery and glassy, and soon she is overwhelmed by the need to vomit. Running to the bathroom, she makes it in time. Figuring it still must be the effects from last night's episode before Philip arrived, she peeks out the door, back into the bedroom, looking to see if she disturbed his sleep. He is still knocked out asleep with the covers down to his waist. After vomiting again, the nausea passes. She gets ready for work, but this time, she has a little pep in her step with feelings of her childhood love.

Completing the morning ritual, she walks out of the bathroom to find Philip standing there naked.

"You know, we can go one more round before you leave and go to work," he says.

"Philip," she says.

"What?" He extends his arms to her.

"You need to get your clothes on. I have to go to work now; we can't do that this morning," she says with a smile on her face.

"All right," he says as he heads to the bathroom. "But you weren't saying that last night, were you?"

"Okay, okay," she responds, laughing. "You need to hurry up so I am not late to work today. I don't want anyone asking any questions."

"Just tell them you had to tend to your business this morning," Philip says, hollering from the shower.

Walking out of the bedroom, she says to herself, "Yeah, that will sound real good. I was getting my groove on with the preacher last night. Yeah, right." Continuing to prepare for work, she gets her stuff ready and sets it by the door to the garage for a speedy exit, still keeping with her time schedule and morning routine. Fifteen minutes sweeps by quickly. When Philip finishes he comes out. Rebecca is standing in the foyer waiting for him. He walks over, embracing her once again, giving her a hug and quick kiss. She smiles, returning the hug.

"You know, this felt so right. Like it was meant to be," he says, whispering in her ear while in the embrace.

Feeling out of sorts and kind of awkward, Rebecca really doesn't respond to what was just said, with thoughts dancing around in her mind. *Could this really be? This is too good to be true.* Then she breaks the embrace. "Okay, I have to get outta here, or I am going to be late for work, man.," she says, rushing him out.

"I see that, but I know you have always been dedicated to whatever job you have had," he says while walking to the garage with her. Kissing him on the cheek, she bids him adieu, notifying him that she will talk to him later throughout the day. In the quick shuffle of getting out of the house, walking to his car, and getting in, he shouts, "I love you."

Giving no response, she moves swiftly to her vehicle, in a state of unbelief at his words. Surprised, she just couldn't say it back in return.

four

The workday for her is in full swing already as she handles the share of duties in rounds. Walking around, checking different charts on patients, making sure all is in order, Rebecca gets a little dizzy and falls up against the wall. Nurse Tiffany grabs her and asks if she is okay. Shaking her head, she tells Tiffany yes.

"Yeah, I'll be all right. I was a little sick this morning. It will pass."

They continue to walk down the hallway, back to the front desk of labor and delivery, and then suddenly Rebecca collapses again, this time passing out. Tiffany hollers her name, going down to her knees beside her to check her pulse. The nurses behind the desk rush to her aid. All working together and pick her up and put her in one of the empty rooms. Tiffany says to one of the nurses her heart rate seems kind of fast, by checking the pulse on her neck.

"She might be dehydrated. Let's gets some fluids going," Tiffany says.

One of the nurses at the desk called her friend Grace, she rushes over from the infant neonatal intensive care unit to see what was going on with Rebecca.

"All right, ladies. Does anybody know what is going on with her yet?" Grace asks.

"She told me that she was a little sick this morning. So I figured we'd start some liquids in case she was dehydrated," Tiffany explained.

"That's good. What's her heart rate at?" Grace asks.

"Seems like her heart was beating pretty fast when I checked her pulse at her neck," Tiffany responds.

Grace examines her by opening her eyes with her fingers, checking pupil dilation. Rebecca is still unresponsive after a few minutes. Grace has them take some blood from her so they can run a few tests and see what's going on with her.

Ten minutes pass. Finally Rebecca starts to come to. Her vision is a blurry at first; then it starts clearing up. A few figures are standing over her, looking at her with concern. Rebecca's focus comes in sharply.

"Rebecca," Grace says, "can you hear me?"

Rebecca looks at her with her eyes squinted, getting ready to respond.

"Do you know where you are, Becky?" Grace continues with questions.

"Yeah, of course. I am at work. What happened?"

"You passed out, Becky. You have been unconscious for a little bit. I took the liberty of ordering some tests and put a rush on them. I didn't think you would mind," Grace says with concern.

Grace looks around and asks those in the room if they wouldn't mind stepping out so she can talk to her privately.

"What? What is it? What's wrong?" Rebecca says, propping herself up with her arm.

After shutting the door, Grace comes back around to Rebecca's bedside.

"What? What is it, Grace? What did you find?"

"I don't know if you are going to take it as good news or bad news," Grace says. Looking directly into Rebecca's eyes, she says, "You have a passenger with you, girl."

"What are you talking about?"

"Girl, you pregnant, that's what," Grace responds.

Sitting up quickly Rebecca asks again, "What did you just say, girl?"

"Uh, you pregnant. That's what I said. I'll say it again. You pregnant, girl."

"I can't be," she says, shaking her head. "I have been taking my pills like clockwork. I can't be."

"You all right?"

"I was a little late, but I thought it was just stress or I was a little ill." Rebecca says, looking at Grace in unbelief.

"Well, I guess this is as good a place if any to find out, huh?"

"I can't believe you just said that, girl. This is not a joking matter. I can't believe it."

Grace looks at her and tilts her head to the side, "Well, I just have one question. Who is the father?"

A chill starts to go up her spine at the utter thought

of who the father of the baby is. She doesn't want to answer the question of who the father is because she knows that Grace will give her a hard time, and this is not the time to hear any lectures on her mistake.

"Let me just take a wild guess, girl. It's Jacob, isn't it?" Grace says with understanding in her voice, to Rebecca surprise.

Rebecca's eyes begin to tear up as she stands up from the bed, putting her head on Grace's shoulder.

"It will be all right, Becky. You know I got your back. Whatever you need, I am there for you," Grace says, hugging her.

Tears continued to flow down her cheeks; her mind is flooded with so many thoughts. First and foremost, being a single mother. She has thoughts of her longtime love and the relationship she has started over with him. Baby daddy drama is one thing she has always tried to avoid in her life. How is she going to break this news to her family, her mom, even worse, her father? Philip, how in the world is she going to be able to tell him this horrific news? He seemed to come at the right time in her life. She thinks of maybe trying to pass the baby off as his, knowing that he wants a family anyway, but she knows she is already to far ahead. So many thoughts rush through her to where she can't process them. In her heart she knows she can't do that to Philip because of their history together. Then she thinks of having to confront Jacob and tell him of the child that she is carrying in her womb is his and his reaction to that news. Then she thinks of just ending the pregnancy to avoid all of this turmoil, but abortion is something she never agreed with. Just the thought of dealing with Jacob on this matter turns her stomach. Lifting her head off Grace's shoulder she says, "I'll be all right, Grace. I'll figure it out and get through it."

"You don't have to do it by yourself. You know you have me and Darrell, Becky," Grace says with empathy.

Rebecca gets herself together, knowing she will have to deal with the other nurses because she is sure that they all know of her condition.

She still can't believe the news. She tries to figure out words to say in her head of how to tell Philip that she is pregnant, thinking that he will probably want nothing to do with her once she tells him she is carrying another man's child. She picks up the phone and dials Jacob's cell phone number, hoping that he won't pick up. While his cell phone continues to ring, she puts it on speaker so she can talk to him. The voice mail answering service picks up on his cell phone.

"Jacob, I know you know my number when it comes up on your cell phone. It is important that I talk to you real soon. Call me back either on my cell or at work when you get this message," she says, pressing the button to cut off the speaker phone, hanging up. Then she calls Philip, and he picks up immediately.

"Hey, girl. I was just thinking about you with your sexy self. It's good to hear from you already," he says, laughing. But there is an awkward silence on her end of the phone. "Bee, is something wrong?" Philip asks.

With tears still streaming down her face, she

purses her lips. "No, nothing's wrong. I just need to talk to you later on, that's all," she says, trying to hide that she is crying.

"All right. I'll be at your house later on this evening after church," he answers.

Hanging up the phone, she puts her hands over her face, mentally beating herself up for the mistake that she has made. All the praying that she has been doing now seems to be in vain because the last thing she wanted was to be single and pregnant. She also never wanted to be tied to someone that didn't want to be with her.

Constant thoughts of regrets and possibilities flood her mind. The prospect of the life now living inside and being a mother to someone overwhelms her. She exits the break room so she can get some air and try to sort some things out, she passes the nurses' station desk. Melissa, one of the nurses, looks at her and asks if she is all right. Rebecca informs them that she is all right and is just taking a little stroll to the nursery. Strolling through the hallway, she touches her belly, thinking, *This is what you deal with every day. It really doesn't matter that you have conceived before marriage. Women all over the world have made a successful life being a single mother.* She tries to keep her mind filled with positive thoughts to encourage herself to go through with having the child despite the circumstances that have come about. Arriving to the nursery, she leans her head up against the observation glass, just looking at the new lives, lying there waiting to be lavished with love and security by their mothers. After standing there for a few seconds, she goes into the nursery and is greeted by one of the nurses.

"Hello, Rebecca. How are you doing? Is there anything I can do for you or help you with at all?" the nurse says.

She just smiles, shaking her head no, and then says, "I just wanted to look at these beautiful babies."

As she walks through aisles of glass bassinets, her mind clicks with a final decision. *I am going through with it. I am going to have this child. I may not have this chance again. Who knows, with me being almost thirty years old?* The silence is broken as one of the infants in the nursery cries, and she picks the baby up. Immediately the infant is comforted by her touch, and Rebecca says to herself, *Yeah, I can do this. I can do this.*

Another hot scorching day has come to a close in the grand ole state of Tennessee, and the evening darkness slowly spreads over the beautiful skies throughout the cities. This is one day that will always be remembered by Rebecca. She takes off her scrubs and puts on some comfortable clothes to go home. Turning over to the night shift RN, she begins to exit and runs in to her friend Grace.

"Hey, girl. How are you feeling?" Grace asks as she puts her arm around her shoulders, giving her a squeeze.

Grace and Rebecca giggle; then Rebecca responds, "I'm doing good. I'm going to make it through this. I mean, look at how far I've come already."

"Only through God's grace and favor. So what are

you planning on doing tonight?" Grace asks as they enter the elevator.

The doors shut to go down. Grace presses the button. Rebecca leans up against the wall in the elevator, looking up to the ceiling. "Well, I gotta give the news to a few people that are a part of my life. God only knows how that is going to be. I am meeting with Philip at my house tonight."

Grace's head turns. "Isn't that the guy you told me about that you were planning on marrying a long time ago?"

"Yeah, that's him," Rebecca says, placing her hair behind her right ear with her head tilted down.

"Since when did he come back into the picture?" Grace asks as the elevator doors open to the lobby.

"About two months ago, the day of the date with Craig and Darrell," Rebecca answers.

"You mean to tell me that you have been seeing him for two months, girl? And you didn't tell me. Have you said anything to Craig about it?" Grace says with a concerned tone in her voice.

"No, it really hadn't occurred to me to say anything to him about it because we only had lunch four or five times together on occasion. It really hasn't escalated to anything else because I think he got the feeling that I was seeing Philip when he showed up at the hospital. He is more like a friend now, even though he is fine," she says as they are approaching their vehicles in the parking lot. Dr. Craig Lowe pulls up where Rebecca's truck is, blocking it, waiting on her. Grace bids her good night.

Dr. Lowe gets out of the car, standing in front of his car door. Rebecca approaches at a steady pace.

"Hey, Craig. How are you? Coming in for the night shift?" she asks.

"What's up, Rebecca? Yeah, it's night shift time again, but the main reason why I stopped by your car is I wanted to ask you a question," he says with a serious look on his face. Rebecca eyes shift to the side, and she says, "Oh, Lord" under her breath then gives eye contact as he begins to talk.

"You know that we have been having lunch on and off. I was wondering if—"

Rebecca interrupts by putting her hand in the middle of his chest. "I know what you're going to ask, and there is nothing more I would like to do than go on another date, but the way things are right now, I just wouldn't be able to, and it wouldn't be fair to you. I have some things going on right now. I am sorry."

"Well, what is it? I am sure it isn't that major. I really would like to see you more often."

She walks over to her truck and opens up the door as he continues to walk behind her. "Just move the car, please, Craig. It is complicated," she says.

"What? What is so bad?"

"I'm pregnant, okay? That's it, and I am already seeing someone. You're a good guy; you don't need to be saddled with someone like me, man. You've been a good friend. I don't want that to be spoiled, okay?" she says, placing her hand on his shoulder.

"I am truly sorry. I didn't mean to push or pry.

Well, actually I did, but I just thought ... I am sorry, Beck," he says apologetically.

"It's all right," Rebecca says, putting her hand on his right cheek. "Still friends?"

"Of course. I wouldn't have it any other way with you," he says, giving her a gentle hug.

Craig goes to his car to move it, pulling into the parking space; then he goes into the hospital. She gets into her car, preparing to drive off, she says to herself, "Boy, can a sister catch a break? It's coming from everywhere. Seems like trouble is following me."

The drive doesn't seem long with all the things racing through her mind of how things will pan out. Pulling up to the house in the driveway, heading toward the garage, she sees Philip waiting in his car in the driveway. When she opens the garage door, Philip gets out of his car and comes in through the garage and waits for her by the door. Once the truck is parked, she steps out of the truck. "Can you get my bags, Phil?" she asks.

"Sure, Bee. No problem," he responds.

Walking over to the passenger side, he gets her stuff out. "You all right, Bee? You sounded really weird over the phone today." Philips asks, walking behind her. Unlocking the door, she opens it. Entering the house, she turns on the light, not really saying anything, trying to figure out how she is going to tell him this devastating news of her unexpected passenger. Still walking in front of him, Rebecca tells him to put the bags down by the door entrance. Philip continues to follow her, wondering what she wanted to talk about. Still walking, she goes to her bathroom and shuts the door. Philip stands there, leaning on the door while it's shut.

"Well, Bee, I'm waiting," he says.

The toilet flushes. He backs away from the door, and it opens. She looks at him as if someone has just passed away from the world. "You should have a seat. We need to talk," she says as they walk over to the sitting area of the bedroom.

"I really don't know how to tell you this, Philip," she says as she puts her hand on his knee and they sit on the loveseat in the room.

"Bee, just say it, unless what you have to say is hurtful and devastating. What, do you not want to be with me anymore. Is that it?"

"It's not that, Philip. You know that I care for you deeply, but I found out something today that shook the very foundation of my world."

Philip starts to frown and says, "Are you sick, Bee?"

"No, but I will be throughout the days to come. I don't know how to put it, so I will just say it. I am pregnant," she says, feeling weight lift from her.

Philip becomes pale, gets up from the loveseat, walks over the bed, and plops on the bed, sitting in shock.

"What did you just say?" he says.

"I said that I am pregnant, Philip," she says, softly awaiting his response.

"How? I don't understand.," he says.

Hesitantly, she tells him by kneeling down to him with her hands on his knees.

"The baby is not yours, Philip," she says, shaking her head while talking. "Although I wish it was. Then this wouldn't be as hectic it is. I was seeing this guy Jacob on and off for some time and got caught up with him one night over two months ago, but this happened, before I knew you were back in town. Before we even started seeing each other again, because had I known you were here I would have been set on seeing you, sweetheart." There is complete and utter silence in the bedroom. Philip's head is down, and his eyes are closed.

Rebecca moves her hand off his knees to his hand on the bed to hold it. "Philip."

He lifts his head up and looks into her eyes and says, "I can't believe this, Bee. What am I supposed to do? How am I supposed to react to a blow like this?"

Her eyes break contact with his. Looking down, her hair falls in her face, and she speaks softly to him. "Love me, that's all."

He moves the hair out of face and says, "I already do, but how do we deal with this situation of a baby? Does the father even know that you are pregnant?"

Shaking her head no, she responds, "I haven't had a chance to talk to him yet."

Philip lifts her head up by touching her chin. "Do your parents even know yet?" he asks.

"Philip, I just found out today. You're the first person I have told. So now I guess you're going to leave me, right?"

"Bee, come on now. How you gonna handle me like that? The next thing is how are we going to explain this to the church? I can't claim the child as mine own. I am not saying that we should stop seeing each other," he says.

"I am not asking you to claim the child. I accept my responsibility and the mistake I made," Rebecca says as she stands up quickly and takes a few steps back, turning around with her back to him. Standing there on the dark-colored hardwood floor in the bedroom, Philip stands up, reaching out to her as her back is turned.

"I am not trying to hurt you, Bee, but how is this going to look to the church with me being a preacher and you being pregnant?"

Rebecca turns around quickly and says, "What did you just say? As much as I love you and want to be with you, I can't believe you just let that come out of your mouth! This probably wouldn't even be an issue, preacher, if it had of been your baby, huh? You weren't thinking about this when you were lying in my bed with me, huh, preacher!"

"Bee, that is not what I am trying to say," he says, walking slowly up to her, but she backs away from him.

"Don't touch me, Philip. You just don't know how low you've made me feel, as much as I've done in this relationship to make you feel that I need you and want you," she says, starting to cry.

"Bee, don't overreact," he says, still trying to embrace her.

"Don't tell me not to overreact, and I said don't touch me," Rebecca says in retaliation.

"Okay!" Philip says in loud voice. "I am trying, Bee. I am trying, but you're making it hard."

Then Rebecca walks over in the sitting part of the room and speaks. "Trying? All I asked you to do is love me like I love you because of our history together. Maybe you don't love me the way I love you."

Philip folds his arms. "Bee," he says in frustration. "What do you want me to do? I am trying to sort through this like you are."

"No, you're not," she says with a little Southern belle drawl. "You're just tryin' to make sure you're in the clear. With you being a preacher, making sure your image isn't tainted." "It's typical with you church preachers, you want to make sure you look good on the outside but you're all jacked up on the inside."

"Bee, what are you saying? What? Do you want me to leave, is that it?" he says. A shudder comes over her body as he says that, and her eyes get big. "Is that what you want me to do?" he asks in a threatening manner.

Reluctantly, she answers, "Is that what you want to do? All I asked you to do is love me, but you make it seem like you can't even do that."

Then he turns around and walks out of the room. Her hands come up to her chest, and she runs after him and shouts to him, "Philip, where are you going?" But he continues out the front door and then drives off without saying a word. Continuing out of the house, she goes to the round, bricked porch with columns in the front of the house, not believing that he is actually leaving and shouts his name again as he continues to drive off. Putting her hand over mouth, she begins to cry and then turns around, going back into the house, shutting the door, falling back on it, sliding down to a sitting position, and crying. Beginning to feel despair, she thinks, *What else could go wrong in my life right now?* She crawls over to the table by the foyer and gets the cell and tries to call Philip. The phone rings but with no answer from him. She leaves him a message, begging him to call her, saying that she didn't want him to leave and asking him to come back.

Hanging up the phone after her message, she heads to the kitchen, dragging her feet across the hardwood floor, walking at a slow pace, feeling sad and lonely, now more than ever. Placing the cell phone on the island, hoping that it will ring and be Philip, she turns to open up the refrigerator, standing there looking in front of it, staring. Bending down, she takes some fruit from the fridge and puts it in a strainer. While running the fruit under water, cleaning it, her cell phone rings. She drops the strainer in the sink to answer the phone, not even looking at the caller ID. Answering without hesitation she says, "Hey."

"What's up, girl?" a voice says, and her facial expression immediately changes, knowing who is on the other end of the line.

"Hello? Are you still there?" the voice says.

"You finally decided to call me, huh?" Rebecca replies.

"What's up with the hostility in your voice? I am returning your call because you said that you needed to talk to me," Jacob says.

"How come you just left and didn't call me or anything?" she says in anger.

Jacob replies, "What are you talking about, girl? That's been over two months ago, I had to go and be up early because I had to take care of some other things that morning. I had other pressing business that was more important. You know how it is."

Rebecca just has an utter look of disgust on her face at his comment.

"Whatever. Well, here's the thing. That night we spent together after the dinner, when you were so eager to see me, a child resulted from that night," she explains. Then she hangs up the phone, looking at it in her hand; then she walks into the family room, her plate in hand to sit and eat before she goes to bed, but now the phone rings. While popping an apple slice in her mouth, she looks at the caller ID, not Philip, but Jacob. She doesn't answer; she continues on with her night and then goes to bed to keep herself from getting too excited and upset about all of the night's drama.

five

Through all the toils, snares, emotional ups and downs of the situation, Rebecca manages to continue on with the everyday routine, despite the relationship shambles that she has created for herself. Looking beautiful as usual, the pregnancy seems to be agreeing with her. Two weeks have passed; she still has not heard from Philip. The very one that she wouldn't think would keep calling has been calling, but she hasn't answered any of the calls or returned them. While in the hospital at work, she has to attend scheduled doctors' appointments in regards to the pregnancy. Who should she happen to bump into at the hospital with her back turned? Rebecca freezes in shock, thinking of the fact that she hasn't confronted the issue or said anything to this person about her pregnancy and then tries to turn around and go out. The person calls her name. "Sista, what are you doing here?"

Rebecca turns back around. "Hey, sista. How are you doing and feeling today?" Rebecca inquires.

"Did you know that I was going to be here today? I don't remember telling you," Paige asks with a suspicious look on her face.

Paige waddles over to a chair in the lounge wing of hospital dedicated to women's health. Once Paige sits down, Rebecca checks in and walks toward Paige. Checking her out, Paige notices a change in Rebecca's shape. Rebecca comes and sits by her sister. Paige looks at her intensely. Rebecca looks at her and says, "What?"

"Is it something that you want to tell me, sista?"

Rebecca just looks at her, unsure of what to say, just being in awe that she would even meet up with her sister at this time. Paige says to her, "You have the look, girl." Continuing to question her, she adjusts her position in the seat, wiping the sweat from her forehead, awaiting an answer from Rebecca.

"What look are you talking about, girl?" Rebecca replies, trying to play dumb.

Paige looks at her rolling her eyes slightly. "Don't play stupid with me, sista. You have never been able to lie to me or keep anything from without me finding out some way. Now, are you going to tell me you are pregnant, or do I have to wait until the baby is born?" Paige says with a smirk on her face.

"You know what? You are a mess, girl," Rebecca says, shaking her head and laughing with her hand slightly over her mouth.

Paige continues to keep eye contact and says, "Well?"

"Okay, okay. Yes, I am expecting," Rebecca confirms.

"I knew it!" Paige says loudly. "When are you going to tell Mom and Dad?" Paige asks.

"I haven't, and you don't say a word," Rebecca says, touching Paige's shoulder.

Then the nurse calls Paige's name. She struggles to get out of the chair; Rebecca helps her up. Then as she is waddling to the back, she turns around and says, "We ain't finished talkin', sista. I will call you this evening. Okay?"

"All right, sista. See you later," Rebecca replies.

Then Rebecca sits back in the chair, making herself comfortable. Her cell phone vibrates. She pulls it out of her hospital lab coat with her legs crossed, leaning back in the chair. Looking at the caller ID, she goes ahead and answers the phone, speaking softly in the lounge. "Hello? Can I help you?"

"Have you lost your mind or something? I have been trying to reach you for weeks, girl. Why haven't you answered my calls?" Jacob says in frustration.

The nurse comes out and calls Rebecca's name to come back for her appointment. She scooches to the edge of the chair and says to Jacob, "I am sorry; I can't talk now." She hangs up the phone with Jacob still talking on the other end.

About two hours have passed. The appointment is over, and she is on her way back to the labor and delivery wing of the hospital. Holding on to a few things, along with reading pamphlets on pregnancy, she does not know that she is being watched as she crosses through the lobby of hospital to the elevators. He waits and watches to see if anyone is going to get in the elevator as she stands and waits. The elevator opens, and she walks in. A man rushes to catch the elevator and puts his arm in the door. Rebecca is startled at the action. The elevator doors open back up, and Jacob walks in and turns to press the button for the door to close. Then he looks at her. "All right now. You don't have choice but to talk to me, Rebecca," he says with his arms crossed.

Standing in the corner of the elevator, she looks at him. "Okay. What do you want me to say? As much as I wanted to be with you, Jacob, you continued to dog me, and for the life of me, I don't know why I let you do that. Maybe because that is what I have become accustomed to, letting those that I get involved with, just do me wrong, but I am tired of it. Now, here I am standing today, pregnant because of a bad choice I made."

"So what are you telling me? You're going to kill my baby?" Jacob says defensively, walking up to her.

"Keep your distance, brother," she says with her hand out. "I never told you that I was going to end the pregnancy, even though the child's father is good for nothing."

Turning to the side, she breaks eye contact with Jacob, "So what did you call me for then?" Jacob says with a loud voice.

"I didn't ask you to do a thing, did I? I just felt that you should know. It was the only honorable thing to do," she says.

Jacob stands there in silence. His head goes down for a second in thought. He raises his head and says,

"Okay, so what are the chances with you and I as far as a relationship?"

Rebecca laughs in unbelief, thinking of all the times Jacob has done her wrong in the past. She responds as the elevator doors open. "You're kidding, right?" Jacob follows her off the elevator in the passageway, trying to get her attention. She turns around to him, still laughing.

"Why are you laughing, Rebecca? I am serious," he says.

"Oh really? So you're ready to drop your whoring around and be committed to one woman and a child. You're really ready for that? I don't think you are. Besides, you're not thinking of me. All you're thinking of is the baby," she says.

In anger, Jacob says, "How the hell you gonna tell me what I am thinking, Rebecca? I came here out of genuine concern for you and the baby."

"Right now, Jacob, I just don't care, and I'm not even concerned of what you think. I just really don't believe you. I am not as gullible as I used to be. It took you dogging me to get to that point," she says with attitude. Then she walks off. He pauses then catches up to her again.

"It's not going to be over that easy, Rebecca. If you won't let me be involved because of your bitterness, then maybe you don't need this child. I guess I will just have to get an attorney and file for custody of our unborn child," he says in a threatening manner.

This statement throws her for a loop. She expected him to do what he has always done: run. Now he wants to be involved, leaving her puzzled of his intentions. Jacob says, "Now the conversation is over." And he walks off back down the hallway to the elevator. When he makes it to the elevator, the doors open. He looks at her before he gets on the elevator and gives her a nod, fixes his suit, and gets on. Rebecca shakes her head then walks to the unit.

Making her rounds through the unit, she checks the rooms, ensuring the work of the fellow nurses under her charge has been taken care of. Stopping in one of the rooms that is vacant, she looks at the bed used for delivery, and closes her eyes, running her hand from the head of the bed to the end, picturing herself in the coming months. The only thing that is missing from the vision is a man at her side; this breaks her daydream. The room is quiet and peaceful, with the nice wood dresser and incubating unit for the baby and the bathroom door open with all of its arrayed decorations. She looks around in the room and goes to the window and sits looking outside. Looking up to the sky, she thinks, *Lord, there has to be something better than this.* While she is in the room, one of the nurses walks by and sees her sitting there.

"Is everything all right, Rebecca?" she asks.

Rebecca comes out of her thoughts and responds, "Oh yes. Thank you. I'll be fine. Just daydreaming, that's all."

"You sure? You look like something is wrong," she inquires again.

"No. No, thank you. Everything is fine," she says, trying to cover up how bad she is feeling in her spirit.

"All right then. I'll give you an update on the patient when I return," the nurse responds.

"Okay," Rebecca says. The nurse leaves the room. Rebecca arises from the window side and closes the curtains to the room and walks out, heading to her desk in the break room. Passing the nurses at the station desk, she looks at them, "What, ladies?" They all are looking at her funny, as if something is wrong. Tiffany, one of the nurses, lets her know that she has a visitor waiting to see her. Rebecca thinks, *Who could it be?* hoping that it may be Philip coming to see her. Walking cautiously to the break room, she arrives at the door to see him sitting in her chair. "Dr. Lowe," she says in a surprised tone.

"What? Were you expecting someone else?" he says jokingly. "I was just stopping by to check on you to see how you were doing, that's all. We are still friends, right?"

"Of course, of course," she says with a little laugh.

Getting up from her chair, he walks over to her slowly. He takes her hand gently and holds it, running his thumb across the top of her hand.

"Well, it shouldn't be anything for two friends to have a little something to eat together, right?" he asks.

"Sure, that would be great. It will take my mind off a few things," she responds.

He pulls her out of the break room, and they walk pass the nurse's desk. "I'll be back in a few minutes, Tiffany," Rebecca says.

Tiffany looks at her with a grin and says, "Yeah, sure." Then she laughs.

Down in the hospital cafeteria, the two of them sit down for a little bite to eat and begin to talk.

"So, have you been doing okay? I know that we don't usually talk a lot but when I do see you, you always seem so uneasy. Is everything going okay?" he asks.

Taking a deep breath, then exhaling, she looks at him across the little circle table in the huge cafeteria. "I don't know if it would be right to talk to you about my problems," she comments, shaking her head.

"Aw, come on. We're friends. That's what I want us to be. Talk to me. You'd be surprised at what I might have to say, or I could just listen. Sometimes that's all people need," he says tenderly.

Those words hit a soft place inside of her, making her feel even more relaxed. "I just feel so out of control in regards to everything that is going on. From the relationships I have been in and still in. Now, this pregnancy. Everything is just all out of order," she says. "This is nothing my parents have taught me or that I wanted."

Craig just sits there. Then Rebecca touches his hand and asks him, "Well, what do you think?"

He pauses for a second, and his eyes close. She looks at him kind of strangely, waiting for him to say something.

"After listening to a few things you've said, I know you don't know right now of which way to turn or to go. We really didn't have a chance to go into all of this, but I do go to church myself and consider myself to be a good Christian. What I hear mostly in everything you're saying is I, I, I. Rebecca, you can't be in control of everything," he says with strong conviction.

What he says really grabs her thoughts. She feels that these are words of wisdom and knowledge from God.

"God is in control no matter what happens to us. Consider your pregnancy a gift from God. Yes, I know it may have not been conceived in marriage, but everybody makes mistakes. God the Father knows that. All he wants us to do in the situation is to repent for what we've done, turn from it, and move on," Craig says.

Rebecca is amazed, thinking that all this is coming out of Dr. Lowe, the man she went on a blind date with. She sits back and just sighs, looking at him and feeling the weight lift off of her.

"We have to realize a few things. We put ourselves into a lot of situations because we feel we don't deserve better, but I am here to tell you right now, Rebecca, that you deserve better, but you have to know that for yourself. No matter what the past is, leave it in the past and learn how to forgive and move on. Once you release a lot of that old stuff, you'll feel a little bit better and a lot lighter," he says, sitting back in his chair and smiling at her.

"Is that right? Wow, I think I have heard someone say it before, but I just didn't hear it like I heard it today. Thank you," she says, nodding her head. After that conversation, the atmosphere seems a little easier for her. They continue eating and engaging in friendly, relaxing conversation until the meal is complete.

The nighttime has filled the sky with beautifully

arrayed clouds in shades of dark blue, and the stars seem placed so carefully in the sky. Rebecca has left the hospital, en route to her parent's house in Germantown. The air has become cool with a breeze in the September wind, which is uncommon for the south. She has the windows down while driving, looking at the different scenery on the way to her parent's home. The cool breeze brings peace to her as she continues to struggle with how to break the news to her parents. The drive seems long, but at last she comes to the beautifully landscaped community in Germantown.

The neighborhood is peaceful and silent. She remembers all the familiar surroundings and smells of flowers and greenery, which take her back to when she was growing up in this very neighborhood. She pulls in the driveway, which is in the shape of a half circle with an awesome sculpture as a yard centerpiece. Reaching for the key to turn off the truck, Rebecca exhales, trying to get rid of the nervousness. Once the truck is off, she lays her head back on the headrest and closes her eyes, praying within herself for God to give her the strength, for she knows that this is the toughest thing she will have to do. A few minutes go by with her hand still on the steering wheel of the truck; she continues to inhale and exhale with a few tears falling from her eyes. Pulling herself together, she pulls down the sun visor of the vehicle and checks her eyes and face, then opens the driver's side door. Stepping out of the truck carefully, she makes it up to the porch of the house, each step seeming harder than the last to climb.

Once at the door, she opens it and goes into the house.

"Hello!" Rebecca hollers out, walking through the foyer area of the house; then her brother Anthony comes up to her.

"What's up, girl? What are you doing here?" he says.

"I came to see Mom and Dad. Where are they at?" she says, being short.

"Mom's in the kitchen with Paige and the kids, and Dad is in his office working on some Bible stuff; you know him," Anthony responds as he walks to the family room.

Rebecca, following him, asks, "What is Paige doing here?"

"You know how her husband is always traveling and evangelizing," Anthony says with his arms out, gesturing as he continues to walk to the family room.

Rebecca gets suspicious of Paige being there after their surprise run-in. "Hey, everybody," she says as she enters the kitchen.

Her mother, surprised to see her, asks, "Hey, Becca. What are you doing here, baby?" Mother Washington says, moving around the kitchen.

"Hey, sista. How are you doing? You feeling all right?" Paige says before Rebecca can speak, laughing and sitting back in the kitchen chair.

Rebecca looks at Paige with wide eyes and gestures for her to stop. Walking by her, she hits her on her arm. "Ouch," Paige announces.

Their mother states, "I tell you, you two girls, I don't know what I am going to do with both of you."

Her mom turns around from pulling something out of the stove. "Well, baby girl, how was your day? What brings you over tonight?"

"Mmmm. That smells so good. I tell you, I am so hungry right now," Rebecca says, rubbing her belly. "My day was all right. A little taxing, that's all," she responds.

Mother Washington takes Rebecca's chin with her hand and looks at her face and says, "You do look a little bit pale. You might want to take it easy on that job of yours."

Mother Washington continues to prepare dinner for the family. Rebecca breaks a little piece of the chicken meat off the dish and puts it in her mouth as she walks back over to Paige. Rebecca looks out the bay window to the bricked backyard, highlighted with landscape ground lighting displaying the manicured bushes and lights in the pool. Her mother calls to get her attention again.

"So, Becca, you normally don't come over unless you have something you want to tell us or something is wrong. So, baby, what is it? I know we may not have been there all the time, but I always know when there is something wrong with my children," she says with a hand on her hip.

Paige looks at Rebecca and then looks at Momma. Sitting at the marble-gray kitchen table, Rebecca taps her fingernails on the table and then looks at her mom.

"I have some news for you and Daddy," Rebecca says and pauses.

Mother Washington continues preparing side items for the meal, then blurts out to her, "You're pregnant," making eye contact with Rebecca.

Paige and Rebecca look at each other. Rebecca's mouth drops open, and she squints, looking at Paige. Paige shrugs her shoulders, saying, "I didn't tell her."

"No. Paige didn't tell me; the Lord told me. I actually dreamed this not too long ago. But I have not said anything to your father," Mom Washington comments.

Rebecca puts her head down and just shakes her head. "I've made such a mess of everything. I am just at the point where I feel so lost, not knowing what to do. I mean, of course, I am going to have the baby. I just wanted this thing to be right, with a husband and everything," she says, looking pitiful.

Her mother walks over to her and places her hand on her head with compassion and pulls her head to her abdomen and assures, "It will be all right after a while, Becca. You remember our conversation we had, right?"

"Yes, ma'am," Rebecca replies.

Paige has her hand on her knee. "Sista, women go through this every day. Why do you think you're any different? Because you are a preacher and evangelist's daughter? We are the main ones that it happens to because of God's plan for your life," she says, patting caressing her knee.

Their mother turns Rebecca's face to her with her

hands on cheeks. "It's going to be all right," Mother says, reassuring her.

Then Father Washington walks in. "What smells so good?" he says, rubbing his belly. Looking at the reaction of the women in the kitchen, he frowns, looking at each one of them. Then he puts his hands in his pocket. "Okay, ladies, what is wrong? What's going on?"

Mother puts her hands on Rebecca's shoulders. Father Washington looks at Rebecca. "Baby girl, what's going on?"

The question has been asked; he stands there in the kitchen, looking at her. Anthony rushes in the kitchen to see what is going on; Paige looks at him.

"Go back in the family room. Daddy and Rebecca are talking. Plus, you're supposed to be watching the twins for me. Get back in there," Paige says forcefully.

"All right, all right. Whatever. I'm going," Anthony says, walking back into the family room.

"Well?" Father Washington says, still waiting. Rebecca rises up from the kitchen table slowly to walk over to where her father is, around the island of the kitchen.

"Well, Daddy. I have some news that I need to tell you," she says, pausing. "Uh, well I am going to have a baby."

He looks at Mother Washington; then he looks at Rebecca again. "You're w-what, baby girl?" he says, stuttering.

Saying it slowly this time, she responds, "I am going to have a baby."

"What? After how you girls were raised? You're what? Is Philip the father of the baby?" he says angrily.

"Daddy," she says, trying to plead with him.

Interrupting her, he says, "I can't believe it. I just can't believe it!" he says, pacing the kitchen entrance.

Then he looks at her again and just shakes his head and walks out of the kitchen.

"Daddy!" Rebecca screams.

She looks at her mom. Then Rebecca follows him to bedroom, but he has locked the door. She knocks on the door.

"Daddy, come on. Open up the door," she says.

Rebecca starts to cry; then she grabs her keys and runs out of the house. Her mother hollers her name. "Becca!" Rebecca runs out of the house, hurt by how her father reacted to the news of her pregnancy.

Back at the manner of Father and Mother Washington, Evangelist Washington was too late to run after Rebecca. She has already driven off. Paige tries to call her on the phone to tell her to come back but gets no answer. Mom Washington looks at Paige. "I can't believe this," she says in unbelief.

Making her way to the bedroom, all you can hear is the high heels of her shoes hitting the hardwood floor of the hallway approaching the bedroom. Making it to the room, she puts her hand on the knob of the door but calms herself before she enters the room to talk to Father Washington. Once she opens the door, she finds him sitting in his chair with his head down.

"Joseph! I can't believe you! How in the world

could you do that to your own daughter? You know things have always been different when it came down to Becca," she says.

Getting no response from him, she says. "I know you hear me talking to you, Joseph. Answer me."

Then he looks up with his cherry brown eyes, intense as they can be. "Phyllis, we have tried hard and have raised our children to do right and not to embarrass us, as this will do to us. We are a preacher and evangelist in the church. What is this going to look like for us?"

She walks and circles around his chair, then looks at him and puts her hands on her hips again. "For one thing, Joseph, we are not God. We are human, just like everybody else, and our children that we created together are human as well—prone to make mistakes just like everybody else. Remember, our children have our DNA, and that child is grown, Joe."

Standing up from his chair, he walks over to the large window arrayed with deep dark purple drapes.

"Phyllis, we have taught her the right way to go in regards to Christianity. Why would she do something so stupid and against what we preach? She has always been that way. She has a good head for business on her shoulders, but when it comes to other areas of her life, she is just so messed up," he says.

Mother Washington walks over to him and puts her arms around his wide frame and lays her head into his back and speaks softly. "You know, Joe, you and I have been so into the church for so long," she says and then pauses. "So have our children, but we've put a lot of emphasis on going to church and making sure our children seem right before the church with you being the assistant pastor that we really have not paid all that much attention to our children. We have neglected them in a lot of ways."

Father Washington turns around quickly, looking at his wife. "What are saying, Phyllis?" he says.

She places her finger on his lips. "Just hear me out, love. I'm not saying that you haven't been an awesome father and a great provider, just that you weren't attentive when it came to the kids and affairs of the house, and I am as much to blame," she says, looking up at him. "This has produced the children that we have today. God had really dealt with me about that because I am always talking about how much they were doing wrong and need to be saved, and yes they need to be saved. But God has to bring them through their issues first as they create a relationship with him. Most of the time, we as the parents are the very issue that they have to fight through in order to come to Christ."

He sits down on the ottoman. Mother puts her hands on his shoulders and begins to massage him.

"So what I'm saying, honey, just as you preach that Christ looks past the faults of the person and sees the need, you are going to have to do the same thing, my love. This is your baby girl. She's made a mistake and knows it. She knows we are already disappointed, but she still needs us because she is alone in this. We are her family," she says.

Taking her hand, he places it on his forehead and

then pulls her to him with his head on her abdomen. "How could she do this to us?" he asks.

"To us, Joe? No, she did this to herself," she says, raising his head.

Looking down into his eyes with his back up against her still, "You're going to have to talk to her and restore what has been broken tonight, and that is your relationship with your daughter," she says plainly.

"I just can't talk to her right away. Give me some time to process this all," he says, shaking his head.

"All right, Joe. Don't let it be a long time before you say something to the girl," she says, kissing him on his forehead. She walks out of the room, leaving him there still sitting on the ottoman. Walking back into the kitchen, Paige has set the dining room table. Holding her belly, she looks at Mother Washington. "Did you calm him down, Momma? You know how he can get about Becca," she says with a dish in her hand.

"Yeah, I believe I got to him. He heard what I had to say; it's making him think," she says with confidence.

Driving back home to Collierville, Rebecca has done nothing but cry at her father turning his back on her and walking out, leaving her standing there. Pulling up to her house, she sees a familiar car in her driveway. She pulls into her driveway and heads to the garage. Taking her time going into the house, she gets all of her stuff out of the truck. She opens up the door from the garage to go in the house, and Philip is standing out on her front door step in front of the window ringing the door bell. She puts her bags by the door and continues into the house making her way to open the front door.

She opens the front door, "What are you doing here?" she asks.

"I, I just wanted to talk to you," he says, stuttering.

She just looks at him and then looks the other way. "I really don't have the energy for any drama tonight. I have had enough," she says, wiping her eyes as she walks to her bedroom, letting her hair down.

He follows her into the bedroom, but she really doesn't even pay him that much attention. "Bee, are you going to stop and look at me or something?" he asks.

She turns around while in the bathroom, running her some shower water, clicking her nails on the sink, and raising one eyebrow.

"Philip, what do you want me to say? I tried calling you. I wanted to see you, and you have not called me for two weeks. Two weeks, Philip. What am I supposed to say," she says, crying still.

"Just give me a chance to explain. That's all I ask," Phillip says with his arm out, gesturing for a chance.

The water continues to run in the background of the bathroom. Rebecca sits on her stool in her bathroom, taking off her shoes. "I don't even know where to begin, Bee.

"Well, you need to start somewhere because my shower water is running and it is late. I have to get my rest," she says with attitude.

"Okay, okay. I just felt like it was so much to swallow at one time. I couldn't think, but being without you lately has made me feel so empty. I want to be here in your life, Bee. I love you," Phillip says while standing in the doorway of the bathroom.

She looks up at him. "You had to swallow it, you say. I am the one with the life-altering change going on. You hurt me to bring the church into it. It was supposed be about me and you. Or so I thought, but you were so concerned of what the church thought," she says, still upset.

"I know, and I am sorry. I just had to figure out how to deal with it," he says as he bends down to her.

"Deal with it? I still do not understand you and where you're coming from, Phillip. As a couple, you have to figure out things together. That is what a relationship is all about. I am tired of being hurt by men that don't care about anything but their feelings in everything that goes on with them," she says with her voice shaky.

"Come on, Bee. Don't be like that. You know you love me," he says with his arms out.

"Yeah, of course I love you. I've loved you for a long time, but tonight, this very moment, it is not going to be that easy, Phil. You say you want to be with me, but then you demonstrated how you feel about my pregnancy with the child not being yours. I don't have the time for that type of struggle within a relationship." Rebecca speaks with such confidence and clarity. "If you want to be with me, it's all of me, not just a certain part. Now, if you still want to see me, you can call me, but now I would like to take my shower and go to bed for the night, and I am spending the night with no company."

Phillip looks at her and then agrees. She escorts him to the door, and he kisses her on her cheek. Closing the door and locking it, she exhales, for this was the hardest test for her to not to fall into his arms and just go with everything he says. She wanted most of all for him to respect her again. Walking back to her bathroom, she gets in the shower and sits on the sculpted seat and lets the water run down her body, relaxing her. Then she looks at the bottom of her belly with a little bump to it and puts her hand there and massages it. Thoughts and plans run through her head of the new child, most of all her shattered relationship with her father, but she realizes that she can only handle things one day at a time.

six

The days continue to get hotter with sticky humidity in the air, even with it being at the end of the month of September. Rebecca has made an appointment for her and Grace to get their hair done so she can talk and get advice from Grace on all the things going on in her life. This morning has been rocky with the morning sickness, along with having a little pain as her body stretches to accommodate the pregnancy. While she's on her way to her rendezvous point, the cell phone rings. With the hands-free device in car, she answers the phone, knowing who is on the line. "Hello, Jacob," she says.

"Hey, girl. What's going? How are you doing this morning? How are you feeling? You need anything?" he asks.

"No," she says, being short with him.

"What are your plans for the day? I wanted to take you out shopping for yourself and for the baby," he says in a chipper voice.

Rebecca tries to figure out what the catch is to all

this, because their last encounter was not pleasant at all.

"Why would I go anywhere with you, Jacob? The last time you and I talked, you said that you were going to try to take the baby from me by getting a lawyer," she says defensively.

"I know. I know. I was brash and hasty trying to get even, thinking you were trying to keep me away from our child, but I know that you really wouldn't do that. That's not the kind of woman I know you to be," Jacob explains.

"Well, my day is pretty full. I am going to get my hair done and hang with Grace, so I will have to catch you another time, all right? Talk to you later. Bye-bye," she says, hanging up the phone up, not waiting on a response from him.

Arriving at the hair salon, she parks and gets out quickly and gets dizzy, losing her balance a little bit. She backs up to the truck to catch herself, thinking, *It's not easy not being in control of my body anymore.* She takes a minute to regain her stance and walks to the entrance of the shop. Entering the door, she spots Grace.

"Hey, Becky," she says.

"Hey, girl," Rebecca says with a smile on her face.

Walking over to where Grace is sitting, Rebecca takes a seat in the spacious waiting area of the salon.

"What's going on, girl?" Grace says, patting her on her leg.

"It's not easy being pregnant when it is hot all the time," Rebecca comments, sitting back in the chair, arching her back, sitting with her legs open at the knee and crossing her ankles.

"Well, Becky, what's up? I know you, girl, when you need a day out like this. What happened?" Grace asks.

"Well, my father is not talking to me because of the news of the pregnancy. I couldn't believe how my mom understood my plight and everything that was going on with me. Usually it's her tripping about different things; then, of course, she already knew before I had even said—something about how God's got a way of telling on you and uncovering your dirt that you do," she explains.

Grace laughs, saying, "You know what they say, girl. What is done in the dark will come to light, meaning that God knows how to uncover you."

Before they can get more into their conversation, they both are called back to their stylists in order to get started on their hair service. The hairstylist asks Rebecca what she is getting today. "Put my hair up in an updo. I don't want any of my hair down," she requests.

Twenty minutes later, they both have been shampooed and conditioned and now are under the dryer for setting and styling. Their conversation can now continue since they are sitting by each other.

"You know, Phillip had left me and then tried to come back, like everything was all right, like nothing happened," Rebecca says, patting her chest with a damp cloth.

"Did you let him come back?"

"Yeah, so-so. I told him that it wasn't going to be that easy, though. I love him. What else am I supposed to do?" Rebecca comments.

Grace looks at her and shakes her head. "For one thing, Becky. You too easily let people walk all over you," Grace comments.

Rebecca lifts the dryer hood up a little with her hand to look at her in disbelief.

"It's true," Grace continues. "You make it too easy for these men. You, my dear, need to realize who you are and who God made you.

Becoming somewhat defensive, Rebecca counteracts, "Since when have you become so religious?"

"I have always had God. I just don't push what I know and feel on everybody else. I only give my advice and knowledge when I feel the Lord pressing me to," Grace says strongly.

Rebecca sits quietly, waiting for more words from Grace.

"Do you want to hear some more? I mean, this is only going to help you," Grace comments.

"I'm listening to you and taking it in," she says.

"Don't depend on these men. Depend on God, for he is the only one that can carry you through. I know that it might seem rough right now, but you know the Lord saw this down your path and already knew before you did that you would be expecting. He knows what you can handle and what you can't," Grace says, touching her belly.

Tears begin to fall from Rebecca's face as the words spoken give her strength that she needs to continue to face the challenges to come with being a mother and on her own. An hour and a half passes; Grace is finished and is sitting, waiting on Rebecca while she pays her stylist for the service. They walk out of the salon, and who would be waiting on them when they walk out?

"Hello, ladies!" he speaks.

Rebecca frowns and puts her hand on her hip. "I thought I told you that my day was busy and I couldn't go anywhere with you."

Jacob puts his hands up. "Yeah, I know you did. I didn't come to try to take you away. I just wanted bring you something. I bought some things for the baby, that's all. I just wanted to show that I am serious about what we discussed," he says as he hands her some bags.

This throws her for a loop, but she doesn't let her guard down.

"It's kind of early to be buying stuff for the baby. I'm still in the first trimester," she says.

"I know. I am just happy about the baby, that's all," he responds.

Rebecca looks at Grace. Grace shrugs her shoulders, unsure of what Jacob's motive is. Rebecca gives the bags back to Jacob, instructing him to put the bags in her truck. As he walks over to the car, Rebecca looks at Grace.

"What do you think about that, girl?" Rebecca comments.

"I still wouldn't trust him, girl. Just because he's your baby's daddy doesn't mean that he has changed,"

Grace comments as they walk toward her vehicle. "Well, where are we going next?"

"Well, I thought we would do some shopping for ourselves and then get something to eat," Rebecca responds.

Grace gets in her car and turns the ignition to start the air circulating through the car. "I'm following you then, Becky," she says, getting in.

"All right. That's cool," Rebecca says.

Rebecca walks back to her truck after discussing plan of action. Jacob waits for her over by the car. He opens the door for her and gives her a smile, taking her hand to help her in.

"Thank you, Jacob," she says.

"Well, I hope you like what I bought our baby. I figured since you were busy today and couldn't really spend any time with me I'd do this for you and our child." Jacob says arrogantly.

"I had already told you that I had something else to do, but I do thank you for the thought," she says, driving off, leaving him standing there.

The hot and humid day continues with the temperature reaching into the midnineties. At five o'clock the sun is blaring, and the ladies are still on the move. Walking the plazas, they have bought various things for themselves to make it a day of pampering. Grace looks at her watch, informing Becky that she needs to get home to cook dinner for Darrell.

They call it a day, but before they part, Rebecca lets Grace know just how much she appreciates her being there for her in her time of need and for the love and advice that she imparted and shared with her. Both of them get into their vehicles, parting from each other. While Rebecca drives home, a feeling of self-worth comes over her at the thought that she is going to be someone's mother. But most importantly, she starts to realize who she is for herself, that she is someone special that has a purpose and plan designed for her.

Pulling up to the house, Rebecca sees that she has company again. She remembered that she forgot to take the spare key from its hiding place in the case she ever locked herself out of the house, knowing that Philip might use it if he knows its whereabouts. Rebecca begins to go through her mind of what drama is going to come from this encounter with him today. Entering the house, she speaks loudly, saying, "Philip!" She doesn't hear a response from him, but she hears slow music playing over the intercom in the house; she calls his name again and no answer. There is an aroma that fills the air, the smell of luscious barbecue. She keeps walking through the house and comes to the dining area. It is set with an ambiance of class and elegance. Rebecca is speechless, but she still doesn't see Philip. Then he comes out of the kitchen.

"Evening, *ma cherie.* I have been awaiting your return," he says.

"Philip, what is all of this?" she says with a grin on her face.

"If you will follow me, mademoiselle, we have an exquisite dinner for you tonight. I still have your schedule, and I figured with it being your day off from work, I'd come by and cook for you. I saw you were out and figured I let myself in with your spare key and prepare it as a surprise." Philip says, holding her hand, escorting her to her seat.

The table is arranged very neatly. Fresh-cut roses sit in two vases on the dining table for her viewing.

"Wow, this is really nice of you," she says.

"You wait until you taste the meal that I have prepared for you, Bee," he says, pulling a chair out for her.

After seating her, he goes into the kitchen and brings out a beautifully arranged salad. "Oh my God. That looks so good, and I am hungry too," she comments.

The table is decorated with classic silverware and good china, along with candles. Rebecca looks at the setting and thinks as he takes his seat, *I hope he doesn't expect something in return for all of this, because that is not going to happen.*

"You are glowing; you look really beautiful, and your hair looks great too," Philip says.

Rebecca is famished from all the running today. She scrambles the words up to say thank you. The meal continues with little conversation and comes to a close with dessert. After the meal, they make their way into the family room to talk and watch some television. Sitting in the same space of the sectional, she puts her feet in his lap while he rubs and massages them talking to her. Rebecca entertains some of what he is saying, trying not to be stressed by any more drama.

While they are engaging in small conversation,

the doorbell rings. It's about eight thirty in the evening. Philip looks at Rebecca. "Are you expecting anybody?" he asks.

"No, I actually thought I was going to spend a quiet evening alone today. I didn't even expect to see you. It could be my mom, since all the stuff that went down with my dad," she replies.

Pushing herself from off the back of the sectional, she gets up and walks to the door, looks out the window, then opens the door.

"What are you doing here?" she says in a whisper.

"I wanted to talk to you to sort some stuff out," he replies.

"Jacob, you just can't drop by my house unannounced. We don't have that type of relationship anymore. Also, I have company right now," Rebecca says.

"What? You're the mother of my child though," he says angrily.

"Yeah, but that's all it is right now, nothing more," she says.

Philip comes to the foyer area, walking up behind her, putting his hand above hers on the door, opening it. "Is everything all right, Bee?" he asks.

Rebecca looking back at him nodding her head yes, but Jacob blurts out, "Yeah, partna! Everything is cool here. Go on about your business."

Philip moves Rebecca out the way and opens up the door more, flexing himself to fight. Philip introduces himself with a strong voice and puts his hand out for Jacob to shake. Jacob looks at Philip's hand

and puts his own in his pocket. "I was talking to the lady before you interrupted," Jacob says arrogantly.

"Excuse me, if I remember correctly, man, she and I were enjoying each other's company before you rudely interrupted. I believe she was trying to tell you to leave politely," Philip says.

"Jacob, just go. I'll talk to you another time, all right?"

"I am that child's father. I want to talk to you now!" Jacob shouts.

Stepping out, Philip says, "All right now, man. She says she doesn't want to talk to you now. You gotta go." Putting his fingertip in the middle of Jacob's chest, he pushes him from the porch.

"Don't touch me, man! Get your hands off me!" Jacob shouts, pushing Philip.

All of sudden, Philip draws back quickly with his fist and cracks Jacob across the jaw. Falling to the ground off the step, Philip jumps from the porch steps to where Jacob has a fallen and hits Jacob again in face. Rebecca hollers to Philip, "Stop! Philip, stop!"

He lets go of Jacob's shirt, dropping him back to the ground and goes back in the house. She comes out of the house, down the porch, and helps Jacob up off the ground.

"All I wanted to do was talk to you, Rebecca, like we used to do," he says, holding his jaw.

"You don't understand. We are not there anymore, and furthermore, you just can't come over to my house unannounced, even after I have the baby," she says, holding him up.

Jacob doesn't really say anything else. He just looks at her and then walks to his car.

"Just give me a call, and we can talk," he says, getting into his car.

Getting into his car, Jacob drives off. She goes back in the house and closes the door and puts her back to the door, closing her eyes in prayer and whispering, "Lord, have mercy." With her hand on her head, she walks slowly back to the family room, where Philip is sitting. "You all right?"

"Yeah," he says shortly. Picking up on his frustration, she gets an icepack out of the freezer. Coming into the family room with an icepack in hand, she walks past him while he is sitting back on the sectional. Rebecca takes a seat by him, taking his hand, puts the icepack on his knuckles.

"The ice should keep the swelling down," she says, rubbing his hand. "Boy, they broke the mold when they made preachers, especially when it comes to you." She tries to break the tension, but there is no laughter from him.

"So that guy is the father of the baby?" he asks, looking at the TV instead of her.

"Yes, unfortunately he is," she answers.

"How in the world did you get involved with a creep like that, Bee? I don't understand it. He seems so beneath you," Philip says, shaking his head.

"Actually, he is quite successful. He just doesn't know how to treat a good woman, but I fell for his game, which I thought was pretty strong," she responds.

Turning to her, he says, "Do you love this guy, Bee? Because you seem to put up with a lot from him—such as coming by unannounced, even while I am here."

"What are you talking about?" she asks, looking puzzled.

"You know what I am asking you, Bee. Do you still have feelings for this guy?" he asks.

"Do we really have to start this tonight? The evening was going great until the interruption, and I really don't feel all that good," she says, holding her belly.

She tries to get up from the sectional. He places his hand on her arm. "Come on, Bee. Be real with me," he comments.

"You have always been the jealous type, even when we were growing up, Philip. I am with you, aren't I? At one time, yes, I had feelings for Jacob. I even thought I loved him. But I realized I didn't deserve to be treated the way he was treating me. I mean, it was hard at first because that is what I had become accustomed to. Finding out that I am pregnant was not something I was hoping for, to be tied to him forever through a child. But I do respect the fact that he is father of the child I am carrying," she says.

Philip moves to the edge of the sectional with his elbows on his knees and his head down. "How are we going to have a strong relationship with this guy constantly in the mix of things?" he asks.

Rebecca pauses.

"So what are you saying, Philip? I mean, after the

big dinner presentation and all this pampering, now you're questioning if we can make it?" she asks.

Lifting his head up, he looks into her eyes. "I am not saying all that. It just seems the odds are stacked against us. This guy, I can tell still has feelings for you. If he didn't, he does now, regardless of what you may feel about him," he says.

She places her hand on his head. "Every relationship has its challenges, honey. I haven't given you any reason not to trust me now. I have really loved only one person, and that has been you," she says with deep compassion.

"It just seems the typical situation of baby daddy drama. This guy will be linked to our lives forever," he says, looking at her with disappointment.

Still not understanding what he is asking of her, she responds, "Phil, I just can't cut Jacob from the child's life. That wouldn't be fair to the baby, nor would it be right or fair to him. Why don't you just be real and come out with it? What is the real problem? It's because the baby is not yours, isn't it?"

Philip is silent.

"Just you not saying anything pretty much says it all. Man, this is such a waste. I love you, Philip, from the core of my soul. I have never held back in regards to having a relationship with you. God knows if I thought you were going to come back into my life, I wouldn't have even got involved with Jacob. But it happened, and there is nothing I can do to change that. God knows I wish I could. Just like I have heard you preach, there is a purpose and plan behind everything that happens in our lives," she says.

Philip stands up quickly, looking down at her. She grabs his hand with her left and the wrist with her right, looking up at him.

"Please, Phil, baby. Please, I need you; don't go. You know me. I have always loved only you," she says, still holding on to him.

Philip shakes his head. Rebecca stands up and puts her head into his chest, begging him not to leave with the way things are. He breaks the embrace. Rebecca follows him.

"Where are you going?" she asks.

"I need time to think. I need some time to myself, that's all," he replies.

Starting to cry, she becomes agitated. "You need some time. You need some time. I can't believe this. You come over here and do all this, and now you're going to leave just because it's not easy. You know what? You should leave."

Not really wanting him to leave, though, she pushes him away because she feels rejected and tells him to go. While walking out, she shoves him because of his reaction and treatment. Then she runs to her room crying and falls on her bed. Philip gets in his car and leaves.

Lying in the middle of her bed, she continues to cry over the one that she believed was her one true love. Pulling herself up to her pillow, she looks at her phone on the bedside table, debating on calling him. Picking the receiver up, she dials his number, but immediately she gets his answering machine. Putting the receiver back on the hook, she covers her face and begins to cry again.

"Why," she asks the Lord. "Why are things going like this for me? I really love this man. Why would he treat me like this? He is supposed to be one of your chosen preachers. I don't understand. I would have done right by him, Lord."

In the midst of her tears, her belly begins to cramp. Her attention becomes directed to her body, and she becomes fearful of what is happening; she calls Grace.

"Grace," Rebecca says, breathing heavily.

"What's wrong, Becky?" she asks.

"I don't know. I think I might be miscarrying. My abdomen is getting really tight, like I have really strong cramps. I am scared. I don't know what to do," Rebecca says, crying.

"What are you doing right now?" Grace asks.

"I am sitting on the edge of the bed," she responds.

"Are you having any bleeding?" Grace inquires.

"No, I don't see anything. Just the strong cramps," Rebecca answers.

"All right. Go ahead and lie down and breathe in deeply and relax your body. I am going to stay on the phone with you until you feel better. Just try to relax, sweetie," Grace says.

"Okay," Rebecca says, lying down, still sobbing.

After ten minutes, Grace says, "Okay, Becky. No blood or fluid has leaked, has it?"

"No, I just have the pain of cramps," Rebecca comments.

"How in the world did you get to this point? Was it Jacob?" Grace asks in a motherly tone.

"It was Jacob and Philip," Rebecca says reluctantly.

Grace calmly talks to her, encouraging her and taking her mind off the pain until she is at ease and the pain is gone, letting her know that she can't let people upset her, especially since she is carrying precious cargo. No matter how it got there, she is in charge of getting this life into the world safely. Grace tells her to come by the lab in the morning to have an ultrasound done to make sure everything is okay.

Night has passed on, and the morning has come, so beautiful and promising. Already at work on her shift, she has already seen Grace in regards to the cramps. After the checkup, she is informed that she needs to take it easy. She tries to take it easy, sitting back in her chair in the break room. She gets a call from her mother.

"Hello, Mom. How are you doing?" she asks.

"I am doing fine, sweetheart. I should be asking you how you are doing?" Momma Washington replies.

"I am doing all right," Rebecca says, sounding depressed.

"Baby, you sure everything is all right?" Mom Washington asks again.

"Yeah, Momma. I'm all right," Rebecca says quickly.

"Okay, I am not going to press the issue. I just wanted to let you know that your father will try to come by and see you. I just wanted to prepare you. I will be praying for you for whatever you're going through that you don't want to talk about. I love you, baby. Bye-bye," Mom says tenderly.

"Thank you, Momma," she responds, and they both hang up the phone.

She turns her chair to the window and closes her eyes, trying to meditate to get rid of some of the stress before she sees her father. About ten minutes pass; the door slowly opens. The lights are dim, and a soft, rugged voice calls to her. She doesn't hear the voice that has called to her because she has fallen into a light sleep.

"Rebecca," he says softly. He calls her name again; she slowly opens her eyes and focuses on the figure in front of her. Seeing white for a minute, she thinks it's an angel, but realizes it's Dr. Lowe.

"Craig," she says, her voice raspy.

"How are you doing, angel?" he says.

"I am doing fine. As well as can be expected," she responds.

"I just wanted to drop by and check on you. I brought you a little something to eat just in case you didn't have breakfast this morning, plus a little something to put in your fridge for lunch," he says, pointing to the lunch on her desk.

"Thank you so much. That was very thoughtful of you," she says, grasping the bag.

"I hadn't seen you in a little bit, so I just wanted to drop by and check on you," Craig says.

"I am trying to stay stress free right now, that is all," she says, looking down at her bump.

"Yeah, I know you have to protect God's gift," he says, touching her belly.

While Dr. Lowe is touching her belly, her father walks in.

"Oh, excuse me. Am I interrupting anything?" Father Washington says.

Dr. Lowe stands up. "Oh no, sir. I was just dropping in to check on her and brought her something to eat, that's all. It's a pleasure to meet you, sir. My name is Craig Lowe, Dr. Craig Lowe," he says, extending his hand.

"Nice to meet you, son. I am Elder Washington. If you will excuse me, son, I would like to have a sit-down with my daughter," he says, putting his hand on his shoulder.

"Sure, if you will excuse me, sir. Rebecca, I will check on you later," he says.

Dr. Lowe exits the office. Father Washington turns and watches him leave. Turning back around, he looks at Rebecca and has a seat.

"Well, baby girl, is that the father of your child?" he asks.

"No, sir. He is just a friend of mine, that is all," she answers.

There is an awkward silence for a second. Pop Washington looks at her and sits back and then sighs again.

"I would have much rather come to your house and talked to you, but I figured while I had the nerve I would go ahead and do it now. You know I am not that good at apologizing and saying that I am wrong," he says in a macho manner.

"I know, Daddy. I understand," she responds.

"See now, baby girl. I want you to understand. I was wrong for what I did to you that night, walking out on you and not listening to you. You are my child, my blood, and no matter what happens in your life, even if I don't agree, I should still be there for you," he says.

With him being the type of man he is, it's kind of hard to keep eye contact with him. Her daddy has never apologized. Her mind goes back to when she and her siblings were growing up. It was all about what they did wrong and what a disappointment they were. It seems like another wall in a relationship for her with her dad has fallen down. She begins to listen. She usually turned a deaf ear because all he did was preach at them about the wrong they were doing. Returning from that thought, she focuses on what her father is saying. He pauses again to gets his words together.

"I am going to be truthful, baby girl. I am sad and disappointed at the fact that you are having the child on your own, not being married, but I understand that things happen in life. I counsel a lot of people almost every day in the same situation. I just want you to know that I am here, baby girl. I know I always dealt with the spiritual and not enough with the natural when it came down to dealing with all of you as my children. But I want to break that cycle right now," he says.

Tears begin to roll down her cheeks again in relief as she sees that her father is compassionate to her problem and situation.

Pop Washington stands up from the chair and walks over to where Rebecca is and touches her hand and then holds it, pulling her up out of the chair. She goes limp in her father's arms, feeling safe and secure.

"I am so sorry, Daddy, that I have disappointed you. I have messed up my life so badly," she says.

He holds her tight, bearing her burden in that moment.

"Baby girl, everybody makes mistakes that they feel they can't recover from. But there is nothing that the Lord can't bring you through if you just trust in him. Also, you have your family too. I know you didn't really feel that way before, but I am letting you know now," he says, still holding her.

He rocks her side to side. She cries and wipes her eyes continually. He continues to comfort her and reassure her that it will be all right. After their meeting is over, she walks her father down to his car. Having one more situation dealt with helps her feel a bit lighter. Before her dad gets in the car, he embraces her one more time and tells her that he loves her and that she is one of a kind and special in every way. She shuts his door, and he drives off, beeping his horn.

It seems that her step has changed. The sky seems a little bit brighter as she walks to the hospital lobby. She sees some baby items in the gift shop; she goes over to have a look. Her mind is not wrestling anymore with mom and dad issues; the only thing that plagues her mind right now is Philip's silence. As she stands there holding an outfit that says "Momma's Boy," someone walks up behind her and whispers over her shoulder.

"You finding what you need?" he says, laughing.

Turning around, she sees that it's Dr. Lowe again. She hits him on his arm.

"You scared me," she says, chuckling.

"You were in another world. I told you to not worry about stuff. Things will take care of themselves," Craig says, putting his hand in the middle of her back, escorting her out of the gift shop.

As she walks with Dr. Lowe to his office in neurology, he continues to talk.

"How did it go with your father? It was nice meeting him," he says.

"We got a chance to get some things out on the table about my pregnancy and everything else. It seems like everything is coming together," she says.

"I told you that God would work it out for you," he says, walking beside her.

"Yeah, you sure did. Now if this man could fall in line, that would be even better," she says, sighing.

Dr. Lowe doesn't really say anything. She looks at him to see what his reaction is. They make it to his office, and she sits on his couch, and he sits on the other end.

"Well, have you ever thought that maybe these are not the men that God has for you?" Craig says. "I don't get to go to church all the time because of the hospital hours and demands, but I do have a relationship with the Lord. Sometimes the things that we get aren't meant for us, even if they're all dressed up, looking like they're handmade for us. Most of the time, that's where the problems lie because we are looking at the outside shell of what we want and not what God wants for us."

What he says catches her attention and makes her think, but she still thinks of the love she feels for Philip.

"What if you are just so in love and you can't stop loving that person? I can't imagine my life without him," she says reluctantly, knowing that Dr. Lowe might still have some feelings for her.

"You need to ask God to deliver you and free you from the relationship if it is not for you. You don't want something that God hasn't designed for you," he says.

Nodding her head in agreement, "You're right, man," she says exuberantly.

He gets up and closes the door to his office. Rebecca feels uncomfortable. Standing up, she asks him what he's doing. He puts her at ease.

"If you don't mind, Rebecca, I would like to pray for you and your situation," he says in a calm voice.

"Oh, okay," Rebecca says in relief.

"Angel, you can trust me. I am not going to hurt you. I want to help you as a friend," he says tenderly to her.

Taking both of her hands, he asks her to bow her head and close her eyes with him while he prays. His prayer has a sense of reverence of who God is, allowing his presence to come into the office. The presence of God brings a peace over the office, takes control of the prayer. Going into the hidden things and foundations of her life that had been fractured and broken, the prayer is a release for the Lord to work, destroying bondages of her past and in her mind that keep her chained to low self-esteem. He prays for God to break every shackle and hindrance that would keep her from entering in purpose and promise for her life, to deliver her from every bad soul tie that would keep her from going forward. Rebecca becomes weak under the presence and power of God. The prayer and concern of Craig has touched her deeply. From the prayer that was offered, a seed has been planted in her life to help her think a little clearly now.

seven

Four months and a few weeks have passed; it is now February. Rebecca is still on the move in spite the different issues that have occurred in her life thus far. Rebecca is well into her second trimester, almost hitting the third one of her pregnancy, showing her big bump really good. It has been pretty rocky for her in carrying the child; her blood pressure has been kind of high due to a lot of stress, but she continues on. Her friendship with Dr. Lowe continues to be a pillar of salvation and strength for her. The relationship with Jacob is on good ground as of right now, and she is being civil to him.

Whatever she has asked him to do in regards to support, he has done without complaint, anticipating the birth of his child. Her relationship with Philip has been rocky; they have continued to talk with each other, though she is doing her best to try to keep things together. He doesn't show that much interest anymore, but she still hopes they can be together. They have met a few times. The soul tie that she has with this man has really hindered progress in her life. Mostly, that is why the pregnancy has been so hard as she tries to do whatever she can to get Philip back in her life fully.

It is unusually warm for wintertime. The bright, brazen sun is still in the sky, slowly setting so that the night can come forth and bring some type of cool breeze through the land. The workday for Rebecca has come to an end. On a whim, she decides that today she will try to make it to church since she hasn't been going that much, due to problems with her pregnancy. She hopes to run into Philip since she hasn't really seen him as much as she used to with him being very busy at the church with other things. She goes to one of the staff locker rooms and freshens herself up, taking a shower to cool down. Looking down at her belly while showering, she is amazed that this experience of carrying a child is really happening to her. It takes a little longer than usual to get ready for her today since she's a little winded and lethargic. Figuring her blood pressure is probably up, she has a seat on the bench to take a little rest, putting some powder on to keep herself from sweating as much. The locker room is empty. All she can hear is the public announcing system of the hospital outside the door. Though it is February, it is still warm, and she puts on her roomy sundress to be comfortable. Finally, after a while, she has gotten herself fully dressed. When she begins to stand up, her abdomen tightens. She thinks, *Wow, I must really be tense.* She exits the locker room and gets to her vehicle: she makes it to church.

The church is kind of packed tonight for Bible study. I wonder what is going on. Getting out of the vehicle, walking slowly, breathing hard, and continually feeling more tired, she eventually makes it to the church entrance. Looking around to see what is going on, she sees a bulletin and reads there is a guest preacher for the week. Reading the bulletin, she sees the series is Building a Strong Spiritual Foundation. The praise and worship music is playing inside the sanctuary from what she hears standing in the vestibule. Walking to the double doors, she is met with a few cold stares. Not paying them any attention, she continues to walk into the sanctuary. Quickly finding her a seat in the middle at the end of the pew, she puts her stuff down. She stands a few minutes for praise and worship and then sits because she feels overly tired. Sitting back, she lets out a big exhale of exhaustion, wiping her forehead with the towel. One of the ushers that knows her comes by and asks her if she needs anything. Sitting back on the pew, she shakes her head notifying the usher she is fine. The service shifts to the choir singing, and the overwhelming urge to use the restroom overcomes her; she gets up from her seat and goes out to the restroom. Coming out of the restroom, her eyes try to process what she is seeing. Rebecca has to take a double take of what she has laid her eyes upon. Leaning up on the wall, she sees some young lady under the arm of who she thought was her man, Philip. Philip doesn't see Rebecca, and the young lady he is talking to intently doesn't see Rebecca either. All that's within her begins to crumble at the thought that the man she has loved for so long seems not to want to have anything to do with her. Her footsteps become shaky as she starts to walk toward them, wiping her eyes; her heart is pounding and racing within her, full of pain and rage. She finally walks up on them and folds her arms on top of her belly.

"Excuse me if I am interrupting something important," she says.

Philip turns around, surprised to see her. "What are you doing here, Bee?" he says.

The young lady interrupts. "Bee? Who are you?" the young lady speaks with her hand on her hip.

"I am his woman, that is who I am!" Rebecca says, breathing fast and with frustration.

"I don't think so," the young lady responds. "I have been seeing Philip for the past month and plan on getting married."

"What?" Rebecca screams. "I can't believe this."

"All right, all right, ladies. Tanya, just go into the church. I'll handle this," he says, putting his hand in the small of her back. The young lady turns to him and fixes his suit and tie, then leaves.

The hallway corridor seems hazy to Rebecca as she tries to process what is going on. She looks at him without words.

"Bee," he says, reaching out and touching her arm.

Snatching her arm back from him, she moves.

"Don't touch me. I can't believe you would do this to me, Philip. What have I done to deserve this?" she says with tears rolling down her face and her chest heaving.

"Look, Bee. I didn't know how to break it to you.

This relationship was just not going to work between us," he says.

"This is all because something happened before you came back. You're just going to give up on us?" she says, still trying to plead her case to him.

Then world-shattering words are uttered from his lips.

"Rebecca, there is no us anymore," he says coldly.

"What do you mean there is no us anymore? I have done everything you could have ever asked me to do. Now you're just going to kick me to the curb?" she asks, continuing to cry.

"I am sorry that it couldn't work between us," he says.

"I can't believe you call yourself a preacher, a man of God, his servant. You're not his servant being like this. You're acting like the pure devil, a hypocrite to the core of your being," she says in retaliation.

"All this that you're saying is not going to make me feel bad and bring us back together. It's done; it's over. I don't want you anymore," he says cruelly and walks away.

Left standing there in complete and utter awe, she places her hand on the wall and puts her hand over her mouth and cries uncontrollably. It seems like time has just stopped and been put on pause in all that surrounds her.

The center of her being feels as though someone has just taken a sledgehammer and demolished everything within her soul, the whole foundation. Thoughts run through her mind of why. *Why do I even try if everything is going to bring me agony?* Her legs become very shaky and weak; she staggers as she heads back to the sanctuary. Her breathing becomes more labored, and her belly begins to tighten severely. She places her hand down at the bottom of her abdomen, massaging it to relieve some of the pain, feeling a sudden drop on the inside. Her vision begins to blur. Suddenly she feels something trickling down her leg. She makes it to the sanctuary, opening the door. Once opening the door, she looks down at her shoes and sees blood on them. Immediately Rebecca passes out in the sanctuary. A scream goes throughout the church. Rebecca's mother runs over to see who has passed out and discovers her own daughter lying there with her dress and shoes stained with blood. The nurse is there on the floor with Rebecca, checking her vitals, hollering out for someone to call an ambulance, to call 911. Philip is across the church with his head down. Her mother is on the floor with Rebecca's head in her lap.

"My baby girl. Oh my god, my baby. Jesus, help," Mom Washington says.

About twenty-five minutes later, the ambulance arrives at the church and begins to take vitals on Rebecca. They look to make sure that she is not hemorrhaging; they find out her mucus plug has fallen out. There is some heavy bleeding, indicating that the placenta has either separated or started separating from her uterus. They try to get vitals on the baby and have a reading of a faint and very low heartbeat. The ambulance races to the hospital with Rebecca and her mother. Rebecca is still unaware of what is going on, unconscious from her very high blood pressure. The ambulance is still racing through the streets to make it to the hospital. The traffic has cleared so that a swift arrival can be made to the emergency room doors. The paramedics call ahead, describing the situation to the emergency room attendees. Arriving at the hospital emergency room, they rush her into the triage unit. The emergency room is buzzing with tense energy, dealing with the situation of having one of their own in need of emergency care. The lights are bright, and it is very busy through every room and corridor of the hospital emergency wing. The attendee doctor on duty does everything within his power to make sure all care and consideration is given. He asks for a portable ultrasound machine quickly to check the progress of the baby.

Mom Washington is in the hospital waiting area, nervously awaiting information of her daughter's progress. She walks outside, holding two purses, Rebecca's and hers. She uses her cell to make calls. Paige isn't surprised at the news, having had been informed already by her husband, who was at the church. Mom Washington closes her phone and looks out at the night sky then closes her tired eyes and prays that the Lord will take care of her child and bring her through with no harm and complete healing. Once she has prayed, she begins to walk back into the emergency room, and Rebecca's phone rings. It catches her off guard. She quickly looks through the purse to see who could be calling. Finding the phone, she answers before the voicemail service picks up.

"Hello, hello?" Mom Washington says quickly.

"Good evening, Rebecca. How are you feeling this evening? I am just calling to check on you," the voice says.

"I am truly sorry, but this is not Rebecca. This is her mother," she says.

"Oh. I am sorry, ma'am. Is she available?" the voice speaks.

"May I ask who is calling?" Mom Washington asks.

"I am sorry, ma'am. This is Jacob, a friend of hers," he says.

"The child's father, right?" she inquires.

"Yes, ma'am. I am," he responds.

There is silence for a minute before Mom Washington tells him that he needs to get to the hospital quickly; informing him that there has been a problem with Rebecca.

He hangs up to rush to the hospital, and Mother walks back into the emergency room to check on Rebecca, but when she gets there, Rebecca is nowhere to be found.

Running to the receptionist desk, she asks, "Um, excuse me. My daughter was just in the room back there, and now she is not there. Her name is Rebecca Washington," Mom Washington asks.

The medical receptionist looks on the sheet to see where she was taken.

"Oh, ma'am, they had to rush her up to the OR," the receptionist says.

"What? Is she okay? What is going on?" she asks.

Not far off listening, a nurse that was helping Rebecca comes up to Mom Washington. Introducing herself, she puts her arm around Mrs. Washington, informing her that there was a problem with her blood pressure believed to be caused by the placenta separating from the uterine wall, putting her in grave danger, and the baby as well. So they had to rush her to the OR to do an emergency C-section.

Mom Washington responds, "Oh Jesus."

"Everything will be fine, Mrs. Washington. They're going to do all they can. Rebecca is in good hands," the nurse says reassuringly.

The nurse escorts Mrs. Washington up to the floor where the surgery is taking place, leaving her in the waiting room to await the outcome of the surgery.

While Mother is sitting in the waiting room, thirty minutes have passed with no information of what is going on with her daughter. Paige then walks into the room, walking over to sit at her mother's side, rubbing her hand position on the hand rest. She doesn't say anything, but her presence brings strength to her mother. A few minutes later, Jacob rushes into the waiting room, frantic.

"Where is she? Is she okay? Is the baby okay?" he says, breathing quickly with tears filling his eyes.

"Being frantic and loud isn't going to help anything," Paige says calmly.

Time passes, and they are all sitting there waiting for someone to let them know what is going on. To Mother's surprise, Pop Washington arrives on the scene about forty minutes later to support her and to see about his baby girl. Finally, a surgeon comes out to brief them on Rebecca's progress. Father and Mother stand there frozen.

"You are Rebecca's parents?" the surgeon asks.

"Yes we are," they answer.

"Well, she is doing fine now; she is stable. She had some uncontrollable bleeding, but we were able to isolate that. Her blood pressure has come down now, but unfortunately we were not able to save the child," he says.

A shudder of silence and sorrow comes over the whole waiting room.

"He was not alive when we removed him from the uterus. We tried to revive him and give him oxygen, but there was no response. The cause of death was due to a complete separation of the placenta from the uterine wall. I am indeed sorry for your loss," he says, touching Mom Washington's hand.

Jacob falls to his knees, screaming, "Oh my God, no, no!"

Mother Washington buries her head into Father's chest, weeping. Paige sits silently in the chair.

"I am truly sorry. We did all that we could. She will still be able to have children later on, though," the surgeon explains. "When you are ready, you can go in and see Rebecca. She is resting."

He extends his hand and touches Mr. Washington's shoulder and apologizes again for the loss, then walks off. After composing themselves, they go to the room and see Rebecca. It is almost too much for Mother and Paige to see her hooked up to all the hospital gadgets, helpless and unconscious. Mom Washington staggers, as if she is going to faint, walking over to Rebecca's bedside. Placing her hand on Rebecca's hand, she begins to weep more, whispering her name. "Becca, my baby girl." Rebecca looks like a shell of herself, having lost so much blood.

All of them surround Rebecca, praying for strength for the family and most of all for her comfort when she awakes to find that her only child has passed on. Jacob slips out and stops one of the nurses on the unit and asks where the child is. She explains they were waiting on the mother to wake up so they could break the news to her and show her the baby. Mom Washington comes out of the room to see where Jacob is. He informs her that he was asking the nurse where was his son was being kept. Mother asks the nurse if she could bring the child to the room where her daughter is.

"That is not something that we normally do. We wait until the mother is awake," the nurse explains.

Mother explains, with Jacob standing behind her, in a soft voice that she will be in there with her daughter, and she wants her to be the first one that she sees when she awakes, and she will break the news to her.

Back in the room, they wait for the stillborn child to arrive. Ten minutes or so pass; then the nurse arrives with the child in a glass bassinet, wrapped so delicately with a cap on, looking like a heavenly angel. Jacob walks over to the bassinet, peering over it at his son, who looks as though he is asleep, and he reaches down to pick him up, gently holding him in his arms.

Tears flow down his face and he shakes his head. Pop Washington walks over behind him, putting his hand on his shoulder.

"It's not your fault, son. Sometimes in life things just happen like this. There is no explanation for it."

As Jacob holds the child, Pop Washington says a word in committing the child into the Lord's arms, then finishes in a prayer. The hour has grown very late now, and it is time for visitors to exit the hospital, but Mother is staying behind to be with her daughter in this trying time, waiting for her to wake up.

Mom lies back on a reclining chair beside the bed, continuing to ask God for the words of wisdom, love, encouragement, and compassion to help her daughter with the loss.

eight

The early morning has come; the cold rain is falling from the sky, hitting up against the hospital window. Mom Washington is still sleeping. The drops against the window become louder and begin to wake Rebecca. Her eyes are heavy from the sedative and the pain medicine. She blinks, trying to figure out where she is. Turning her head, she sees her mother. "Momma."

"Momma," she calls again.

Mother lifts up her head and looks at her and then goes to her side and kisses her on the forehead.

"Oh, my baby, my baby. How do you feel?" she asks.

"Like a truck hit me," Rebecca comments. "The last thing I remember was my stomach cramping and going into the sanctuary and everything going black."

She reaches for her plump belly, but her belly is flat. Her eyes get big with fear, and she looks at her mother.

"What happened? Where's my baby? Is the baby okay?" she says.

As she tries to sit up in the bed, her mother urges her to lie back down. "Baby, I have something to tell you, okay?" Mom Washington says, holding her hand.

Rebecca shudders and spots the bassinet in the room by the window.

"Is that my baby over there?" Rebecca says anxiously.

"Becca, listen to me," Mom says, interrupting her.

"What, Momma?" she says in frustration.

"The baby, your son, didn't make it," Mother says.

Rebecca looks at her mouth, but the words seem to go in and out for a second. Rebecca asks her to repeat what she just says, hearing *baby* and *not making it.* Mother continues to talk, but everything around her seems to have gone silent. She looks through her mother; then her eyes focus on the bassinet.

"What? What? You mean to tell me that my baby is dead? Is that what you're telling me? That can't be true, Momma; it can't be."

"I am so sorry, baby," Mother says, crying.

Rebecca reaches for the bed control to lift up the bed in a sitting position. Then she asks her mother to bring the bassinet over to her; her heart is pounding so hard in her chest, as if it is going burst through. She begins to perspire a little as her mother rolls the bassinet to her. Her hands go up to her mouth as she sees his little face.

"Oh my God, oh my God," she says.

Placing her hand on the bassinet, her mother looks

on with a sad face, seeing her child going through this tragedy, this situation in life right now, with no husband by her side for support. Mother picks up the child and puts him into his mother's arms. Rebecca begins to weep, holding him close, putting her face on his. Mother sits on the bed beside her and puts her arms around her while she holds the baby. Rocking back and forth with the baby in her arms, crying and weeping, she feels that her world has come to end, that all hopes and dreams she had in store for being a mother have been shattered.

Mom Washington doesn't try to say anything; she just grieves with her daughter. Out of the crying, her mother speaks to her as she holds the still child tightly.

"So, what shall you call him, Becca?" Mother asks.

"His name would have been Aaron Caleb Washington," Rebecca says with tears rolling down her face.

Wiping her face with her hand, still holding him in her arms, Mom thinks to ask her if she is going to put him down, but she rethinks anything that might set her off, further triggering her to snap.

"Becca, I am going to step out for a few minutes and get something to eat. Do you want me to bring you anything, dear?" Mom asks.

Rebecca shakes her head no, not even looking at her mother, fixed on looking at the child so tiny, putting her finger on his chin and lips, examining him. Her mother walks out of the room and exhales, placing her hand on her stomach. Feeling the pain of her daughter, she starts walking to the elevator and sees

Jacob coming up the hallway. She greets him with a hug.

"How are feeling, son?"

"It was kind of a rough night, trying to process all of this, but I made it through. How is Rebecca? Has she woken yet?"

"She has taken it pretty hard, as expected. Be careful of what you say to my baby at this critical time," she says, warning him.

Jacob agrees and breaks conversation with Mom Washington and heads toward the hospital room. As he approaches with flowers in his hand, his steps are slow. He reaches the door and places his hand on the stainless steel handle. Pressing it, the door opens to a crack, and he places his hand on the middle of the door, pushing it open. Sweat is rolling down his head, and his stomach is in knots. Once the door is all the way open, he stands there for a second, looking at Rebecca holding his son. Rebecca looks up for a second and looks right back down at the baby. He steps into the room, and the door closes behind him. He walks over slowly.

"How are you holding up?"

She doesn't answer him, acting as if he is not even there. Jacob speaks again in soft tone.

"Ree, how you doin'? How are you holding up?"

She finally looks at him. "All right," she responds in a real low voice.

Coming up closer, he asks if he can hold his son. He walks the room with the child in his arms, crying to himself. Rebecca speaks again, wiping her face with her head held down. "Aaron."

"What?" Jacob responds, turning around.

"Aaron Caleb. That is his name," she says.

Walking back over to her where the glass bassinet is, he places the child in the bassinet. She puts her right hand out and places it on the glass bassinet, pulling it closer to the bed. He walks around to the other side. Rebecca continues to stay fixed on the lifeless child. He sits on the bed at the end and takes her hand.

"You know, the first thing I want to do is apologize to you because I know that I didn't make things very easy on you. I know that it won't bring Aaron back to both of us, but I want to say that I am sorry. I have been a sorry excuse for a man," he says.

Still fixed on the child, she does not respond.

"Ree, what I am saying is I have realized what an awesome woman I had being with you, and I messed that up, and I want to make things right if I can and do right by you. I have seen the light through our loss, and it has made me a changed man. I want to be there for you in every way."

Rebecca slowly looks up and then turns her head, looking at him.

"Why are you saying all of this now, Jacob? It doesn't change anything. Months ago, I longed to hear those words from you before I had even found out I was pregnant with your son," she says in a calm voice, pausing as tears still flow down her face.

"Now just because of the loss of our child, you

want to try and have a relationship with me again? I'm not trying to be cruel, because I know you're hurting as well, but you had your chance. Now, in a way, I kind of see maybe it was not really meant to be. Even though in some way I loved you, but to try and make something out of it now ... " she says, shaking her head.

Jacob pleads with her, beginning to tear up, asking her to give him another chance.

"Jacob, I have known you long enough," she says, looking back over at Aaron. It would be unfair to start a life with you knowing you and I belong to other people, wherever they may be. You're released through the death of our son; you're released from me and him to live your life free," she says, touching his hand.

As Jacob begins to speak, she reaches over, picking up the baby, again holding him in her arms.

"But, Ree, I don't understand. What are you saying to me? That you don't want to see me again?"

"I don't, but hopefully you are a changed man, and when the next woman comes along, you will know to treat her right. Because when you do wrong, it comes back to you. I still love you. A part of me always will. I wouldn't want to try to build a life with you off this tragedy. I wish you a good life. Now, if you don't mind, I want you to leave," she says, taking her attention off him and putting it on the baby.

Jacob leans forward, putting his head down. He stands up and looks at her. With Aaron in her arms, she looks out window with tears falling from her eyes. He lowers his head and exhales. He leans in and kisses her on her head with tears falling from his eyes. Then he walks to the door, opening it, looking back at her and the baby. No eye contact is given from Rebecca.

"Good-bye, Ree. I love you," he says and walks out with the door, closing it behind him.

Rebecca closes her eyes, and tears fall as another chapter in her life comes to a close. Hours later, she is still holding the baby when a nurse comes in to check on her again. Asking her how she is doing, taking her vitals and checking her stitches, she informs Rebecca that they need to take the baby. Rebecca pleads for her not to take the baby. But eventually she gives in, knowing what must be done. The nurse leaves with the baby. Rebecca is left in the room all alone with the cold silence surrounding her in the room and with the IV dripping and machine going to take her blood pressure and vitals. Turning over on her side, she pulls her knees up as much as she can and closes her eyes. When her eyes closed, all she can see is Aaron. Mom Washington comes back after eating and freshening herself up to check on Rebecca and sees that Rebecca is sleep. Kissing her on her forehead, she looks around to see if the baby is still in the room and no baby. Mom Washington goes out to the nurse monitoring desk and asks the whereabouts of the baby. They inform her that Rebecca allowed them to take him, informing her that they will bury the child and will inform Rebecca where the child is buried.

Late that afternoon, Paige walks into the dark room. Walking over to the window, Paige opens the curtains wide. She comes and sits at her sister's bedside, rubbing her legs gently and calling the name they use for each other.

"Sista. Hey, wake up. Sista," Paige says.

Rebecca slowly wakes up, focuses on Paige, and sits up. Paige embraces her.

"It's okay, sista. That's it, girl. Let it out," Paige says.

Rebecca just lays her head on Paige's shoulder.

"I know that it is hard right now, but you just take it one day at a time," Paige says in a comforting voice.

Rebecca lies back down on the bed, and Paige gets in the bed with her, kicking off her shoes. They face each other as they used to when they were little. With tears still rolling down her face, Rebecca looks at Paige.

"I don't know what I am going to do, I feel like something has died on the inside of me. What is there left to live for?"

"Sista, some days you're going to feel that way. The Lord doesn't expect you to heal from this overnight. Nothing is done overnight, sweetie. Everything has a process," she says, stroking her head.

Mom Washington wakes up and sees her daughters positioned as they were as children and walks over to them.

"Hey, girls," she says. "How are you feeling, Becca?"

"I am doing all right. I got sista here with me now. Go ahead and go home, Mom, so you can take care of Dad and Anthony," she says, touching Mom's arm.

Mom Washington kisses Rebecca and gets her stuff, quietly leaving.

"Thank you so much, sista, for coming, even if it is just for a few minutes," Rebecca says.

"Don't worry. I am here for the night for you. Tyler is with the children; they can do without me for a night. I know you need me," Paige says, rubbing her arm.

"Sista, I just don't understand why. Why would God allow my baby to be taken from me?" Rebecca says, sniffling.

"Sista, I know it's tragic, but we can't blame this on the Lord. Let's be thankful that we didn't lose you. What I do know is that God knows what is best, even though we don't understand all the time what that is. He sees and he knows everything. He has your son right now. Even though he is not with you, he is in the bosom of God. He thought it better that he be with him," she says. Paige continues to console Rebecca.

"The Lord will just have to help me because I'll probably never understand," Rebecca says while shaking her head.

"And that is all right that you don't understand. We will never understand everything that goes on," Paige says while continuing to look into her sister's eyes.

"How did Jacob take it?" she asks.

Rebecca doesn't say anything at first, but she tells Paige all of what happened in regards to Jacob, of how he wanted another chance but she felt it was more of a release for him and told him to go. They continue to lie and talk through the night. The nurse brings food in for Rebecca, but she doesn't pay any attention to the food. They fall asleep talking. Evening passes into morning. Paige wakes up, but Rebecca is still asleep. Paige writes Rebecca a note, letting her know that she had to go get her household together for the day.

Rebecca wakes in the midmorning. Time is passing slowly for Rebecca. The nurses have come to check her and deliver food, but she is not eating. They try to explain to her that she needs to eat so she can recover, but she pays them no mind. One of Rebecca's good friends and staff of the hospital learns of the tragedy and stops by the ward to visit her. Grace asks the nursing staff of Becky's progress. They share their concerns with Grace, that Rebecca has not been eating her meals, giving the excuse that she doesn't feel good. They observe the signs of trying to starve her body because of guilt from losing the child, pointing out the classic signs and symptoms of what they usually see in situations like this one. One of nurse staff comments, and then Grace picks up the chart to look at her progress before she goes into see her.

Flowers and balloons in hand, she goes into the room. The curtains are drawn, and there is no light in the room.

"Hey, Becky. What's going on, girl? How are you?" Grace asks as she enters the room.

Putting the flowers and balloons on the dresser in the room, she then walks over to the curtains, pulling them open. "We need some light in this room, girl," Grace says.

"I just want to lie here, that is all, and be," Rebecca says.

"Well, girl, you know me. I know that you have

lost something that is very precious, but you are precious as well, and we are not going to lose you too," Grace says, pausing for a second with her hands on her hips.

"So what is this that I hear that you have not eaten any of your meals?" she says, walking toward Rebecca's bedside.

"I am not hungry for anything."

"Now, you know I am not going to let you get away with that excuse, Becky. I know you. You're not going to starve yourself because you are depressed. You know me. If we have to force feed you, that can be done. I will put the order in for it if I have to," Grace says.

"Why can't you just leave me alone right now and let me be?" Rebecca asks as she pulls the sheets up to her shoulders and turns over in the bed away from Grace.

"Well, sorry to disappoint you, but I am not leaving you alone to do harm to yourself. For one thing, I am your friend, and real friends tell the truth, and that is why I am here today," she says, pulling the sheets off Rebecca. "Come on, girl. Get on up. You know if you were in my shoes, you would do the same thing. Have you washed up or showered yet?" Graces asks.

Rebecca responds with no. After about twenty minutes, Grace convinces her to get up.

In the bathroom, Rebecca stands there in the shower, letting the water hit her body, not really doing anything; then she sits on the bench in the shower. Grace comes in to check on her. Seeing her sitting there, looking like she has no energy, she helps her by washing her. After that is all done, she has gotten some fresh bedclothes for Rebecca and has food ordered for her to eat. They continue to talk, but Grace administers tough love to her to try and get her out of her depression so she can take care of herself. Sitting there with Rebecca, she watches her play with her food. "You know," Grace says. "Sweetie, you can't do this to yourself," she says, letting her know she is not alone.

Rebecca doesn't say anything.

"I know you hear me, but you don't have to answer me. Yes, it is awful; it's terrible that you lost something that meant the world to you, but you know some bad things happen to us. They happen whether we deserve them or not, and we learn to deal with it, making it part of us. We grow stronger from it, because it hasn't destroyed us or who we are, but it defines us. I am going to continue to check up on you, Becky. Don't let this destroy you. You hear me?" she says, sitting on the bed. Grace hugs Rebecca and then gets up off the bed and goes out of the door to the nurse's station and tells them to continue to keep a close eye on her and alert her if anything happens.

Rebecca sits in the room alone, pondering everything that has been said to her. While she is crying, the door opens, and the figure almost looks like an angel of light, but it's Dr. Lowe there to check on his friend, his angel. She is surprised to see him, especially at this point in her life. He comes in with two dozen white roses and brings them to her bedside.

"Oh my God. Thank you so much. They're beautiful. Thank you," she says, smiling.

Craig sits on the side of the bed to talk to her.

"What are you doing here?" she asks with a smile on her face, touching his hand.

He smiles at her tenderly. "I heard what happened, angel, so I had to come and see how you were holding up and if you were up for company," he says.

She tilts her head to the side and smiles, responding, "Of course from you. I am holding up. I feel everyone praying for me."

"You know I am praying for your healing, not just in your body, but in your mind and spirit as well. This is a pretty devastating blow to your life, but I want you to know that I am right here whenever you need me," Dr. Craig responds.

"I feel like such a failure. It's all my fault. I'm a nurse; I knew better. I knew that I was stressing, causing my blood pressure to go up, not controlling it. I was asking for it," she says.

Craig stops her before she goes any further, punishing herself, by putting his fingers on her lips. "You're not a failure just because you miscarried. Things happen in life that we have no control over whatsoever, but people deal with it and move on and become stronger."

Rebecca still tries to blame her past actions that caused her to lose the baby. Craig continually thwarts her negative thoughts, trying to keep her encouraged and not put guilt on her shoulders.

"Angel, I know with being a nurse working in the

labor and delivery that you've dealt with many cases that have ended up where you're at right now. God forbid it happened, and there is nothing that we can do to change it. All we can do is just trust and believe that God will carry you through this and give comfort and peace. You know I am praying for you continually. Even in your loss God is still able Rebecca," he says.

"But I just don't understand why. Why would God take my son from me? I thought that he was a God of love," she says.

"God knows the future, angel. You may have been spared from other types of situations or pain that you may have not known was coming. You told me you were having problems with the men in your life, especially your son's father until recently. As horrible as it may sound right now, this could have been an escape for you from years of tribulation. Who knows but God? God has a blessing in store for you. Just hold on, angel. Your darkest hour is just before the break of day."

The words don't make much sense to her right now as she deals with the grief and frustration she feels at the moment. The nurses have also informed Dr. Lowe of her starving herself. Through the continued conversation, he lets her know that he cares for her very much and doesn't want her to cause pain to her mind or body due to something that was beyond her control. It's a struggle for her to receive the words that could bring comfort and freedom from the chain of guilt; she still is in despair.

"I know that you may not be receptive to everything that I have said, but believe me. Each day here after will get a little bit better for you. Anything you need at all, you just let me know, angel, and we'll make sure that you have it because I want you to get better. Okay?" he says, patting her hand.

She nods her head in agreement to his request. He begins to get up from the hospital bed, and she holds on to his hand; he looks at her.

"What is it, angel? Can I get you something?" Craig asks.

Rebecca responds to him, still holding his hand while he is standing by the bedside. "Can you please do me a favor, Craig?" she asks.

"Sure just name it," he says.

"I really don't want to be alone right now. Can you just please sit with me a little longer and hold me, please?" she asks, beginning to cry.

"Sure. I'll sit with you as long as you need me to," he says, sitting back on the bed.

She lays her head on his lap, feeling his strength, love, and concern for her, along with a sense of safety. Craig stays there and holds her until she drifts off to sleep. When she is asleep, he whispers a prayer for strength for her to go through this time of grief and come out of it stronger than she was before.

• • •

Words of knowledge, power, and encouragement have been spoken into her life to help sustain her through the loss of her child. A few weeks later, she has taken leave from the hospital in order to recuperate from the surgery. She is trying to use this time to get her head together as she deals with the depression that haunts her from the loss of her son. In the beginning, after getting home, it was very difficult for her to cope with seeing all the different baby items she had started to accumulate. To her, the house feels so empty and cold, missing the presence of the child. Still not having much of an appetite to eat anything, she knows that she is going to have to face packing up all of Aaron's stuff. In that time being home, much to her surprise, there have been many frequent visits from the good doctor to make sure she that she is eating right. He made her meals, serving her and keeping her company, encouraging her to battle against the depression in her mind, not just for her life, but the life lost. Dr. Lowe continues to give her nuggets of wisdom and compassion to help aid in her recovery of overcoming life's adversity. Through the time spent together, he gives her building blocks in natural as well as spiritual to build a firm foundation in her faith, confidence, and strong self-esteem to help her throughout each day.

It's midmorning, around ten o'clock on a Tuesday. Craig stopped by already for the morning; he has continued to make it part of his daily routine to check on her before he goes to work. Rebecca is still at home, having finally gone through the baby clothes for Aaron, boxing all the items up and placing them in totes for storage. Finishing that difficult and emotional chore of going through the baby's stuff, she feels torn. Having gotten through it, there is a weight lifted, but then, on the other hand, there is despair there in the depths of her soul. The doorbell rings, catching her attention. She is still walking kind of slowly from the stitches from the C-section surgery. She makes her way to the door. Looking out the peephole, she sees that it's her mom and Paige. Opening the door quickly, she greets them with hugs and affection. "What are both of you doing here?" she asks.

"Sista, now you know better. We are coming to see about you like we've been doing. Have you eaten anything yet this morning?" Paige says, walking through the doorway.

"Yes, warden. My friend, who is a doctor, comes by and checks on me to make sure I am eating. I am doing a lot better than I was," she says, walking with them through the foyer area.

Mom inquires what she was doing before they came. Seeing the baby clothes in totes, Mom Washington doesn't say anything else. Rebecca informs them that she is going to stow them away. Paige and Mom look at each other.

"Becca, with all due respect, baby, I think you should store these away. You shouldn't keep them. Give them to Goodwill or something. That's just a bad memory to have around," Mrs. Washington says.

Rebecca is disturbed by her mother's suggestion. Paige steps in quickly.

"Sista, you don't have to do that right away. I just think what Momma is trying to say is the past will bring haunting memories. Don't hold on to it. No rushing it, though, baby sis. Take some time, you know, girl," Paige suggests.

Even the suggestion from her big sister does not sit well with her, but Rebecca lets it roll off her. At first she thinks to react to what she feels is pressure to let the memory of her son go. She restrains herself, thinking, *Why would they both say that, knowing that I just lost my little boy over a week ago?*

They are in the cabana room, where most of the baby stuff is located, and music is playing softly in the background.

"Sista, I am proud of you, though, how you have gotten through the task of going through all of this baby stuff by yourself," Paige says. "You do have strength that is God given, Becca, because I don't know how I wouldn't have done it if it were me.

As Mom and Paige have a seat in the cabana room, Rebecca goes over behind the bar, walking slowly, and gets them something to drink out of the cooler.

"Is your C-section scar healing well?" Paige asks.

"Yeah, they did a really good job. It shouldn't leave that much of a scar," Rebecca says, rubbing her hand across her belly.

Mom Washington looks at her. "Have you heard from Philip?"

Rebecca, drinking her water, brings her glass down slowly, looking at her mother.

"No, I haven't, and I hope I never hear from that hypocrite. He is one of the reasons why I lost my baby," she says, feeling rage on the inside.

Paige and Mom say, "What?"

"How is that possible?" Mother says.

Then Rebecca goes into how she caught him talking with some other female in the church hallway, all close to the young lady, explaining that, to her amazement, he and the young lady had been seeing each for a few months and had a plan to get married. Going back over the story of events triggers some emotions in her, but she continues to explain how they got into an argument, and when it was over, he walked away from her. Then she woke up in the hospital, finding out that she was not pregnant anymore and her son had passed away.

"Oh my God, sista. That is awful," Paige says.

"He walked out on me a few times because of the thought that the child wasn't his, saying, 'What would the church say about the situation?' It was a hot mess. All I thought about was how I could please him because I didn't want to lose him. Instead of thinking about me and my child, because of my foolishness of running after him, I lost my baby and sense of myself, and there is no changing it," Rebecca says, turning her head and wiping tears away from her face.

Mom Washington walks to her and wipes her daughter's face. Then she lifts her face, softly telling her, "Despite what you went through with that young man and the things you've seen in the church, don't let that affect your relationship with the Lord. Allow him to heal you from the inside out, Becca."

Paige looks at Rebecca, making eye contact with her, nodding her head in agreement with their mother. Paige tries again to talk to Rebecca about relinquishing the baby stuff she has bought. After careful thought, she agrees to let Mom and Paige take the stuff from the house. They continue their visit in pleasant conversation, changing the subject from tragedy to something joyful. Rebecca informs them that she will be going to his gravesite to pay respects and everything. They agree in her endeavor to put this behind her and move on; it's more easily said than done, though.

After they leave and she is in the house alone, her home phone rings. She lets the answering service screen the call while she is watching a movie. The machine makes the beep, and she mutes the television to hear who it is. A male voice on the answering machine sounds like someone very familiar. She picks up the phone slowly and cautiously. "Hello?" she says.

"Oh you are there. I was wondering how you were doing," the male voice says, sounding a little shaky.

"Who is this?" she says sharply.

"It's me, Bee," the voice says.

She feels sick on the inside after recognizing the voice. "Why are you calling me, Philip?" she says with disgust.

"I heard in church your name on the prayer list and what is was for, and I just wanted to apologize for what happened and for your loss," he says.

"I can't believe you have the nerve to even call me after what you did to me? If you didn't want to be with me, that is all you had to say instead of leading me on and seeing someone else," she says angrily.

"I did try to tell you many times, but you begged me to stay and not to leave. I didn't want to break your heart, and I still had feelings for you. I couldn't just leave you at the time," Philip says.

"I don't want to hear it, Philip, You shattered my dreams and broke my heart. Because of you, I lost my son. I hope you get back everything that you dished out, and that it comes to you ten times worse, you hypocrite," she says.

Then she hangs up and exhales with tears rolling down her face. Reliving the emotions and the drama of the incident with him, she curls up on the couch, putting one of the pillows under her head, and she finishes watching television until she falls asleep.

nine

Rebecca awakes to a new day. Every time she wakes up, she looks down at her flat belly, which almost seems to be a dream that has turned into a nightmare that she cannot wake from. But the scar that she bears on her body serves as a haunting reminder that indeed the nightmare is reality. She lifts herself off the couch, her head hanging down. Knowing that she has to face another day, she lifts her head up to the ceiling as if she is looking for the help of the Almighty. Through her mind, she thinks, *Why not just sleep each day away,* since losing the baby. Dragging her feet, walking into bathroom, she turns on the water to take a bath and try to get her mind together. She figures this is going to be one of those days that will drag on with nothing but depression in front and behind it. Then the phone rings, and the answering machine picks up; it is her fellow coworkers. The nurses call to leave her a group message that they are thinking about her and missing her presence.

The bathwater is still running. She continues to

gather her things in preparation for her bath, thinking about what she can do today, in order to keep her mind from constantly thinking about Aaron. Slipping off her robe, she slides into the tub filled with sudsy water, and aromas of sweet-smelling lavender, chamomile, and vanilla fill the bathroom. Soft music plays through the house on the intercom as usual. She closes her eyes, taking deep breaths in and out, as in meditation, while sitting in the steamy hot water. Doing this, she tries to exhale all of the negative energy out of her body and into the atmosphere. She drifts off into a light sleep from the meditation, to a relaxing place in her mind. She can feel the presence of the Lord surround her while she is in meditation, helping her through the pain and dealing with her depression. With his presence surrounding her, the Lord begins to minister to her soul and mind telling her, *I know your loss was great, bruising you to the very core of your soul, just as I lost and gave up a son for you and this world. I am asking you to let go of the pain. Let me have the first-born. Know that your son is resting in my arms, with no pain anymore. Now move toward the blessing that I have in store for you.* With the comfort of the Lord's spirit and words of wisdom he has spoken to her spirit, she knows that he is there and he is keeping her through this time of pain and suffering.

Two hours later, she has finished with her bath, gotten dressed, and cleaned up the house a little and is getting ready to sit down and watch some TV in the family room. The doorbell rings unexpectedly. She thinks it might be her sister or her mother again, checking up on her, but when she opens up the door, much to her surprise, it is Dr. Lowe.

"Craig. What you doing here?" she says.

He has flowers in his hand and a picnic basket.

"I come bearing gifts. May I come in, angel?" he says with a pleasant smile on his face.

Rebecca does not hesitate to let him in, smiling and laughing at the flowers that he has for her.

"I guess these are for me?" she says, smiling.

"That is correct, my dear," Dr. Lowe responds while they stand in the foyer.

Rebecca beckons him to follow her while she puts the flowers in some water. "So what are you doing here? Not that it isn't nice to see you."

"I took the day off. You were on my mind, so I figured I'd stop by and get you out of the house for a little bit. You know, hang out together. I have a basket for an old-fashioned picnic. The weather isn't all that bad. It's kind of nice and warm for end of February. You up for it?" he asks, touching her hand.

She willingly agrees. "Let me go and change into something else, if you don't mind," she says.

Craig nods to her. Quickly, she goes into the room and gets herself together and throws on something nice.

While driving, Craig looks at Rebecca with affection as she looks out the window. When she turns to look at him, he quickly looks straight through the front window. The day seems to very pleasant with the smell of Southern winter in the air. As the air is blowing in through the windows of the car, she turns her head to him.

"You just don't know how much I thank you for checking on me and taking care of me since I have been down. I don't know how to repay you for all of your kindness to me," she says sincerely.

He just smiles. "It was no problem at all. In fact, it was a pleasure to wait on you and take care of you. You are well worth it, angel," he says, looking straight out the window.

They pull up to a beautiful park with children playing and trees blowing in the calm winds. "We are here, angel," he says as he parks the car.

She begins to reach for the door, and he tells her to sit there for a second and gets out of the car, walking over to her side and opening up her door. He puts his hand out for her to take, which throws her off but impresses her. They start to walk slowly through the park, looking for a spot to take a seat. They spot a perfect spot underneath a tree. The place is so perfect; it looks as if it were taken out of a picture.

They stop underneath the tree. Before they sit, he asks Rebecca to hold the basket while he spreads the blanket out on the grass. Snapping the blanket in the air, he brings it down to the ground through the blowing air, spreading it out, making sure that it is flat on the ground. Taking the basket from her, he helps her to sit on the blanket. While she is sitting, he takes bug spray out of the basket and sprays the perimeter to keep the bugs away.

"You have just thought of everything, huh?" she says, smiling.

He laughs. "I just wanted this day to be relaxing

for you," he says, continuing to set items up for the picnic.

While he is on his knees beside her, prepping everything, her mind starts clicking, and she lowers her head. She then looks at Dr. Lowe. "Why are you doing so much for me, Craig? I've done nothing to deserve this from you," she asks.

Still preparing the picnic, he looks at her and tilts his head to the side. "You're special to me. That is why I do what I do for you with no expectation of anything in return. I believe you're an extraordinary woman," he says.

Again, he takes a few more things out of the basket, placing them in front of both of them. She goes on to say, "I have done so many things wrong in my life that have brought me to the point of where I am right now, and I don't feel really good about myself."

Craig exhales slowly, looking at her gently and seeing in her the beauty of a queen, and speaks. "It doesn't matter what your past is and what you've done. Your past is a learning tool; it doesn't determine who you are. It's not set in stone. You have a choice, angel, to let it make you or let it destroy you. And I know you are stronger than what you think," he says.

His confident words catch her attention and cause her think.

"Angel, you really don't know how special you are, do you? You radiate beauty, intelligence, grace, and humbleness. That is what I admire the most about you. You're confident when it comes to your job and wherever else you're placed. Even though sometimes you're not very sure of yourself personally, you excel in your work in every way. Even when you told me you were pregnant, I never stopped caring for you because you are indeed a treasure that is worth finding," he says.

She slowly lowers her fork, listening to the words coming from his lips, hanging on to every word as is if her life depended upon it. After words so heavy in thought and insight, Rebecca is lost for words, so they continue to eat in silence of the moment. Rebecca's mind continues to process everything he has says, but what she can feel the most is his concern.

Rebecca looks at Dr. Lowe and breaks the silence. "You know, all this time I used to hate when my mother and father would try to preach to me when I was growing up. I thought they were just trying to keep me from having fun, granted, yes I think they could have done some things different. But I don't fault them because they felt they were doing right in what they knew. Now I see the things you have said to me in the past and even now are working to help me in so many ways; I don't even have the words for it," she says.

"Like the Apostle Paul says in the Bible, I planted, Apollos watered, but God gave the increase," he says, being witty.

"That is from the Bible, right?"

"Yes, angel, it is. You know, a lot of the truths that we live by are the precepts and examples given from the Bible; we just don't know them for ourselves," he responds.

"You know, when I first met you, I never would

have taken you to be a true man of God. I thought you were just a fine-looking, well-bred gentleman who was spiritual," she says.

Craig leans back on the tree that they are under, looking at her and smiling. "I feel that I don't have to put on a front or show when it comes to my Christianity or relationship because whatever is on the inside of a person will come out. One thing I always try to keep in mind, though, is not to make the Lord Jesus ashamed of me. I want to be pleasing in his sight. People never realize that sometimes your life will be the only Bible that people will ever read when you profess Christianity," he says, continuing to eat.

Holding her plate and looking at him, she finally feels a genuine connection for the first time with anyone. She really doesn't know how to act on it, having just gone through a relationship with someone that was supposed to be in the church, but evidently the church was not in him, and the relationship was about lust instead of love.

"You know, Craig, everybody talks such a great game, but their lives in the end never reflect what they talk about. You know that I just came out of a relationship. I really don't want to bother you with this," she says.

Craig interrupts. "Go ahead. You can tell me anything."

She continues. "The relationship I was in was with my childhood sweetheart. I really thought that he was going to be the one. I mean, he was a preacher and all, not to mention my father knew him as well. He was very prominent in the church. But he did me wrong. I did everything I could to keep him, everything to make him love me, and he threw me aside like yesterday's trash for another woman who he had been seeing for quite a while when he was with me, just because the baby I carried was from another relationship, which I knew was a mistake. I really don't think I can love again like that. He hurt me so bad, especially with him supposed to be a man of God," she says.

Tearing up a little, she wipes her face, finishes her talk, and looks at him to respond or judge. Still leaning back on the big tree, he pauses for a moment and closes his eyes, breathing in as if he is meditating. He opens his eyes, making eye contact with her, but says nothing. She looks at him, still waiting for him to answer.

"You want me to comment on what you just said? Angel, not everything requires a response. Sometimes it just requires someone to listen to you. This is done so you can release and get some things off your chest and from your life. so you don't carry them anymore. Sometimes you just need a listening ear."

Her mouth drops open, and she stutters, "Umm … umm … so what you're saying is sometimes you just need a friend?"

Craig agrees. After that, she really can't say anything else. The subject changes, and the conversation continues on to other uplifting things. Time seems to fly by. Rebecca is careful even though she knows that Craig cares for her deeply. Three hours have passed by, and the picnic has come to end. They start to pack up all the items and trash.

"This was very nice, Craig. I really appreciate you coming by and taking me out; it was very gentlemanly of you. You really seem to be a true friend. It felt good not having to talk about trying to be on a date or all the relationship stuff. Just regular talking. I haven't had that in a long time, even with Grace," she comments.

"That is what I am here for, a friend that you can trust and talk to you," he says, stuffing the leftovers into the picnic basket.

Walking back to the car, he holds the picnic basket and blanket in his right hand, and she takes his left arm and puts her arm through his, walking with him. More now than ever, she feels that a true friendship has evolved with Craig.

Returning to her home after the lunch date with Craig, she walks into the house. Going over to the table, she sees that there is more than one message waiting on her answering machine; she presses the button. Standing there in the kitchen, listening to the messages, her mind ponders on the pleasant outing that she has had for the day; then the first message plays, and it is from her mom checking up on her of how things are going for the day, wondering where she is. The next is from the hospital notifying her of the change requested by her during her time off, they will be putting her in charge of another unit instead of the labor and delivery when she comes back to work.

She walks to her room; then the phone rings again. She immediately leaps on the bed to answer it.

"Hello!" she says with excitement in her voice.

"Hello, Becca. Where have you been?" her mother asks.

"Oh, hello, Momma," she says.

"Were you expecting someone else, dear?" Mom Washington asks.

"Oh no, ma'am. Did you need something, Mom?" she asks.

"I want you to come over and have family dinner tonight, just like we used to do. Can you do that? Would you be up to it, or are you busy tonight?" Mom asks.

Closing her eyes. "Um … no, Momma. No, I don't have anything planned," she says, biting her lip.

"Well, we will be looking forward to seeing you here at the house," Mom says, hanging up the phone.

After hanging up the phone, she calls Grace because she hasn't really heard from her in a while. Rebecca waits for her to pick up as the phone rings a few times; it's finally picked up. "Hello, Grace?" Rebecca says.

"Yes, this is she," Grace responds.

"This is Becky calling to check in with you," she says.

"Hey, darling. How are you doing?" she says in cheerful voice.

Rebecca quickly responds, "I am doing good. I am making it."

"I know that I haven't called you in a little bit. I

figured that you might want your space right now. I know your family has probably been surrounding you with their love. Have you been eating like I told you to do?" Grace asks.

"Yes, Mother Grace," Rebecca responds and then laughs.

"Where are you at now?" Grace asks.

"I am at home now. I just came back from the most marvelous picnic with Dr. Lowe," she says.

"You're kidding, right?"

Rebecca tells her no, then goes on to explain what a comfort and a friend that Dr. Lowe has been through everything that is going on right now in her life, almost as if he was placed there for a reason. Rebecca goes on to share the details of the afternoon event, informing Grace that there was no pressure to date him or have a close relationship with him, just a genuine, down-to-earth guy friend that listened and didn't overtake her. Grace is pleased to hear the success of her day but also has some news to share with Rebecca.

"Darrell and I finally set a date for the wedding, which is going to be six weeks from now, on a Saturday," she says excitedly.

"Oh my God," Rebecca says.

Grace begins to explain, feeling Rebecca's disappointment of not knowing about the event coming up so soon. Grace goes further to let her know that they had the date set, but with everything that was going on with Rebecca, they felt at the time it just wouldn't be right to talk about it.

Another call comes in after the conversation with Grace.

"Washington residence. Can I help you?" she says quickly.

"Yeah, Bee. How you doin'?" the male voice asks.

"Why are you calling my house? I thought I told you not to call here anymore. We are done, through. You were the one that made that very clear at church," she says angrily.

"Bee, I just want to make everything with us square," Philip says with humility.

"There will never be a chance for us to be friends or anything. You have ruined that, brother. I hope you and your church ho will be happy for the rest of your life. You will get what you deserve," she says, hanging up the phone.

• • •

Arriving at her parents' house as requested, she observes how the weather has changed drastically from earlier. When she opens the door, they shout, "Surprise!" She is shocked completely with a lot of people from the family being there at the house. Rebecca looks around with confusion written all over her face. Paige walks up to her with one of the new baby twins on her hip, asking her if she forgot today was her birthday. Rebecca puts her hands on her head, blown away at the fact that she didn't remember today was her birthday. Having the wonderful picnic and intriguing conversation with Dr. Lowe, she just totally forgot. Her dad walks up to her and gives her a big hug.

"Hey, baby girl. How are you doing? Happy birthday, my sweet girl," he says, hugging her again.

Feeling the love of her daddy's covering through his embrace, just as the Father up in heaven loves, for a moment she forgets about her problems. She holds on to him for a minute. Mom Washington comes along and says, "All right, you two. Break it up; break it up. I know that you probably weren't even thinking about your birthday. I didn't want the day to go by without a celebration. So I want you to enjoy tonight. Okay?" Mom says, hugging her.

Looking around at all the people, seeing that there are cousins, aunts, and uncles that she hasn't seen for a while, she begins to interact with everyone, being polite. The party turns out to be a success. When everyone is leaving, Rebecca waits until everyone is gone, thanking everyone for coming and the presents of love to her. Turning to her mother and father, she embraces them, thanking them for such a wonderful party, letting them know it really meant a lot to her.

Leaving her parents house with presents that were given from the family, she bids them a good night. In heading to the house, she detours and goes over to Dr. Lowe's home. Pulling into his driveway, she sees the house is dark, but lights are on outside of the house. Feeling something rising up in her now, she tries to revert back to her old nature of getting the man she wants. She walks up to his door and rings the doorbell. While waiting for him to come to the door, she fixes her hair by running her fingers through it. She exhales, trying to think of what she is going to say to him. He comes to the door in his boxers and T-shirt with his robe open.

"Rebecca, angel, what are you doing here? Is something wrong?" he says.

"I am truly sorry for stopping over at this late hour, but I just wanted to tell you that what you did for me today ... well ... um ... it really, really meant the world to me," she says.

He asks if she would like to come in. She thinks for a second and nods her head. When she walks in, he comments on how he is sorry the place is a little bit of a mess right now.

"Are you sure that something isn't wrong?" Craig asks.

"You know, out of everything that is going on in my life right now, I didn't even remember that today was my birthday, you know that?" she says, walking up close to him.

He backs up a little. "No, I didn't know that. Man, that is funny, though, with us having the picnic today," he says, smiling.

Walking up closer to him, she puts her hands on his chest and slips them around to his back, hugging him tightly. "Angel, what are you doing?" he says with a strange look.

"What I should have done a long time ago," she says, still holding on to him.

Looking up at him, she kisses him. In return, he begins to kiss her back before breaking the embrace.

"No. No. I, we can't do this. You don't know how much I would love to be with you right now, but we can't do it like this," he says, closing his robe.

Rebecca just looks at him, confounded.

"What, you don't want me?" she asks.

"Of course I do, but I don't want to steal something that hasn't been given properly," Craig says.

"What are you talking about? I am here right now giving myself to you," she says.

With her arms open, she walks into the foyer. He goes after her, grabbing her arm.

"There are a lot of things that you are going through right now, and it just wouldn't be fair to take advantage of that with you. I know you're hurting inside and alone, and if you need me to be there, I am but not sexually. I am a man of God. That is who you got to know and who you see before you. I don't want to taint that image by falling into a night of passion with you. Granted, yes, you are desirable. But it has to be right in the sight of God. I respect you too much to defile you like that. Please understand. You shouldn't be used and abused. You should be protected, cherished, and, most of all, restored."

Rebecca feels ashamed and walks toward the door as he lets her arm go. "Oh my God. I can't believe I just threw myself at you like this," she says.

"Please, angel, don't be angry with me. I care for you deeply. I have nothing but your best interests at heart," he says with his hand on her shoulder.

She opens up the door and walks out of the house, back to her vehicle. Driving home, she continues to beat herself up about the whole ordeal, remembering back to how she used to chase after the man instead of letting them come to her. *Crap. I can't believe I just did that. I'm so stupid. Why did you do that, girl? You know you just came out of a bad relationship. Why would throw yourself at him? How am I going to face him?* Replaying the incident over and over again in her mind, she pulls up to her house and into the garage. Walking in to the family room, she throws her jacket on the sectional. After she goes in to the kitchen to get something out of the refrigerator, she hears the beeping noise, recognizing that it is answering machine. She walks over to it and stands there and looks at it, dreading that it might be Craig on the machine. Reaching her hand out to press the button, she draws it back as if it were hot, in her mind saying, *I know it has to be him. What kind of message has he left on here?* Finally, she presses the button and listens to what he had to say. Lowering her head slightly, she feels even worse learning that he has held up his vow of waiting for sex until he is married. *What could I do to redeem myself?*

Going to her bedroom, she drops her purse on the floor and falls back on the bed, still thinking about the night. Eventually, she is able to stop thinking about the situation so she can prepare for bed. Getting in the bed, she pulls the sheets up and turns over to her side and looks at the phone again and picks it up then hangs it back up and turns off the lights in the room and tries to go to sleep, still troubled.

In the morning, Rebecca is on her way to the hospital to get her checkup again and healing of her body from the miscarriage, thinking, of course, there is a distinct possibility of running into Dr. Lowe in the hospital while she is there for her appointment. Walking through the lobby of the hospital, she sees a lot of familiar faces. She cuts the conversations short, telling them she is trying to make it to an appointment, but in all actuality she is trying to avoid running into Dr. Lowe. She makes it to an elevator with no sign of him. Others on the elevator exit on different floors. She closes her eyes for a minute, trying to settle her mind. The elevator doors open on a floor, and Dr. Lowe steps in with a smile on his face. Feeling another presence, she opens her eyes. *I'm caught.* Before she can say anything, Dr. Lowe speaks.

"How is your morning going so far, angel?"

"I'm all right," she says quickly.

Dr. Lowe starts to talk, and she puts her hand up, saying, "Don't say anything. I feel like such a jerk and ho for trying that on you last night," she says apologetically.

"Believe me, angel, it took a lot of willpower for me not to give in, but I don't want you to feel bad about it. Things happen; we roll with it and keep moving," he says.

While talking, she holds her head down. He asks her if she is even going to look at him. She tells him she can't right now because of how ashamed she feels.

He goes over to her and bends down so he can see her face; then the elevator door opens up to her floor. She gets out without saying anything, and he follows her.

"Just because we didn't make love to each other doesn't mean that our friendship is over. Sometimes you have bumps in the road in different relationships. I am not going to let our friendship go down the tubes. I am not going to let that happen," he says to get her attention.

Rebecca turns around. "You don't know, Craig. I felt like such a fool, like you didn't want me," she says.

"Rebecca, angel, you're a beautiful woman. Why wouldn't I want you? Of course I do, but you don't have to give your physical body for me to feel something for you. You're a prize that any man would love to have, and of course I want you, but I want you to know who you are and that you're somebody. If we are going to embark upon a relationship together, you can't be insecure. Relationships don't last like that," he says softly.

"Why didn't you explain all of this last night?" Rebecca asks with her arms folded.

"Because the whole situation caught me off guard. I was not expecting you to come like that, especially after all that you have been through. I don't want to be the rebound relationship. I want to be the man of God for you that the Lord has called me to be, to be a strength and shield for you. When you are weak, I can be strong," he says, putting his hand on her arm.

Once again he has caught her attention, making her think. For the life of her, she can't figure this man out. Having been in prior relationships filled with drama, all she knows to do is to look for the same thing.

"Is everything all right between us? Can we continue our friendship together?" he says with both of his hands on her arms. Rebecca gives in and starts to smile, knowing in her heart of hearts that this is what a genuine friendship and relationship feels like, someone that is looking out for her best interests and wants to invest in her by building her up instead of tearing her down. He escorts her to the appointment for her checkup, and once that is over he comes back to take her to where her old desk and locker room is. She goes there to clean her stuff out to move to another office dealing with more administrative management since that's what she was doing in the labor and delivery unit anyway, along with duties of being a nurse. Rebecca put in for this change so she wouldn't have to deal with seeing all the babies being born around her as a constant reminder of not having her son. The general staff hospital board weighed the pros and cons of her service and transfer figuring she would be an asset to the new division they were sending her too. The journey to her old unit has been a painful one all the time that she has put into the unit, but she thinks on the positive note that this could be a new start for her. She runs into all her staff that is there when she goes in to the unit with Dr. Lowe with her. Everyone, of course, is sad to see her go. They all say their goodbyes, and she cleans out her stuff and heads to the new job with high expectations.

ten

Five weeks have passed. The day has finally come for her to go back to work, starting a new chapter in her life with a new position and job within the hospital. Now dealing with a trauma and burn unit she walks into her new small office and just stands there for second, looking at the big difference from where she was before. As she is putting her things around the office, someone comes in to remind her that there is a meeting today that she needs to attend. Then in walks Grace to check the new office out and check up on her.

"Hey, Becky," she says, smiling and giving her a hug. "Getting yourself situated in this new office, I see. I tell you one thing, girl, this is something else. The trauma and burn unit isn't that bad. You do have some cases that will touch your heart, just like in labor and delivery, but some of your time will be freed up, though, which is good," Grace comments.

"Yeah, I know. I am just in awe of everything that is falling in place. It's like I am being given a fresh start," Rebecca says while she puts books up on the shelf.

Grace has an envelope in her hand, and Rebecca notices it. "What is that you have there, girlfriend?"

"Oh, this for you. It is the formal invitation to the wedding this coming Saturday. I did keep your dress for you if you wanted to still be in the wedding party," she says.

Rebecca stands there with a blank look on her face and then responds, "You kept the dress? Seriously?"

"Of course I did. We always had you in mind. You know you're my girl," Grace says.

"Of course. Yes, girl, I still want to be in the wedding. It would be an honor," she says.

Grace squares up everything with Rebecca, giving her times and dates for different things in regards to the wedding. Grace is helping her put different things in order, and Dr. Lowe walks in to see the progress in the office. He announces himself to the ladies as he walks in the office. He begins to talk with Rebecca, finding out her plans for the day. Grace can see that there is some chemistry between them and just puts her hands on her hips and looks at them and laughs. They both stop talking to each other, giving the rundown of their schedules, and look at Grace and ask, "What?" at the same time.

"Something has been going on with both of you, hasn't it?" Grace asks.

They tell her that they are just good friends, not really trying to think about a serious relationship.

Grace stands to the side and looks at them out of the corner of her eye, standing by the door of the office.

"Well, since you two are so in depth in your conversation, planning your time for each other, if you will excuse me, I have some last-minute things to do for my wedding, so I will see you both later. Goodbye," she says, leaving.

"Bye," they both say, continuing to talk.

Grace exits the office, leaving them alone. They continue to talk; then her phone rings. She looks at it, picking it up and wondering who would know that she is in her office already. She answers the phone, giving her professional title; the person on the other end of the line needs her to come down to the emergency room to chart in a burn victim. Hanging up the phone, she looks at Craig, informing him that she has to go but would like to get together and sit down for lunch and talk. Acknowledging her suggestion, he quickly leaves out of the office, allowing her to make her way to the emergency unit using the elevator. Making it to the emergency room unit, she goes to talk to the attendee in charge, who informs her that the victim is a child. They had the child sedated at the moment because the burns on the body were so severe. Hearing the news of the case sends a shiver through her body. She asks where the child's parents are, and the attendee informs her that they are in the waiting room and also lets Rebecca know that they have called child protective services already. She nods. With the chart in her hands, she makes her way to the child.

When she pulls the blue curtain back, she gasps in terror of how badly the child has been burned on his body. The nurse attending the young boy looks at Nurse Washington, saying, "Girl, I know. It's awful, a precious child such as this with third degree burns all over his body. He probably won't survive through the night with burns like this," she says, shaking her head.

Rebecca puts her hand over her mouth and steps back behind the curtain, gathering her emotions. Stepping back in the area where the child is, the nurse asks her if she is all right. She nods yes and breathes deeply.

"Well, Washington, I will leave you now so you can get the child ready for transfer up to the burn unit," the other nurse says.

Rebecca shakes her head at the state of the child and puts her hand on the child's hair, caressing him. Then the parents walk in while she is with the child, asking if their boy is going to be okay. She looks at them and introduces herself.

"Hello, Mr. and Mrs. Hamilton. I am Nurse Washington. I will be following the case on your son we have here. As for right now, things are shaky. I can't tell you if he is going to be okay. He has over fifty percent of his body covered in third-degree burns. More than likely, to give you a worst-case scenario, there is a sixty percent chance that he will not last through the night with such severe burns on his body," she says.

Then she begins to ask the parents a few questions in regards to their whereabouts at the time of the incident, where the child was during the accident.

She keeps a professional demeanor but is steaming on the inside at such negligence from the parents. To her, they both seem genuinely concerned; then she lowers the bomb on them, letting them know that since this incident has occurred they had to notify child protective services. Of course, the parents were becoming irate. Rebecca takes a few steps back and informs them if that they do not calm down that the police will have to escort them out. Rebecca informs them that she will now have to transfer the child up to the burn specialty unit for further observation. Observing everything going on today, it looks like this will be a late night for her, but she takes it in stride.

Things go according to plan, and the child is transferred to the burn unit, and the parents are notified where the child is located. Around-the-clock care is being given to make sure the child is comfortable, keeping him sedated. She continually looks in on him to check his progress through the night with this being her first case within the burn unit, also updating the doctor on call. It has gone well into the late evening. Around ten thirty, she gets a visit from Dr. Lowe. Happy to see her friend, a smile comes across her face.

"Hey, angel. I knew that you were going to be working kind of late tonight with this being your first day in this unit. I brought you some Chinese food. If you don't mind, I would like to eat with you so we can sit down together and relax a little," Craig says, holding the bags of food.

Smiling at his gesture, she gives him a hug. They go to her office and sit down and take a break for a few minutes, enjoying each other's company. Rebecca shares with him her encounter today in the burn unit dealing with the case of the child. Also, she talks with him about her going back and forth in thinking of going to school, transitioning over to being a doctor. Craig is amazed and excited at the news of such a huge decision and encourages her that she should be a doctor with all the knowledge and ambition she has for medicine and the heart of caring for the people.

While they are sitting in her office laughing and talking, she gets a 911 page from the station. She excuses herself quickly, leaving Craig in the office, quickly scrambling to the ward where the child is. He has crashed, and the nurses and doctor on call are not able to revive him. *I can't believe that this happened to this poor child,* she thinks to herself. Briefly reminiscing over the loss of her own child, she keeps her composure, trying to stay professional.

"What is the time of death?" she asks the doctor.

The doctor asks the location of the parents so he can give them the news. Rebecca informs him that they are out in the waiting area and that the couple has been reported to child protective services. The doctor leaves after he gives orders for an autopsy. Rebecca goes back to her office to find Craig still waiting but asleep sitting on the couch.

She looks at his strong distinct features and his jet-black hair and medium brown skin with a goatee. She laughs, thinking, *I can't really believe he stuck around for our little dinner date. He really is a dedicated man, better than any of the other men that I have encountered.* She just stares at him, smiling and knowing what a great friend she has acquired in her life. His head is leaned back on the couch with his mouth open; he starts to wake up and sees that she is looking at him.

"Why didn't you wake me up, angel?"

"You were looking so rested; I just didn't want to wake you," she says, still smiling.

She walks over to him. Rebecca, reading his body language, can see he is getting a little nervous.

"Relax. I am not going to try anything, Craig. Do you mind if I sit right here next to you?"

"Sure," he says, moving over a little.

She has a seat and puts her feet up on the couch and gets under his arm a little bit.

"This is not making you uncomfortable, is it?" she says, looking at him.

He shakes his head no.

"Did something happen while you were gone?"

She sighs and exhales, then tells him of the tragic case of the little boy with the burns, taking her back to losing her own son.

"I can't say that I understand everything that you go through because I am not in your shoes. In this job, sweetheart, you're going to come up against many cases that will propel you into a whirlpool of feelings. You will deal with memories of your agonizing loss, but each time you get stronger for getting through it. I am proud of you. You got through this case today because you're strong, and I am sure there are going to be many more."

Looking up at him with her head on his chest, sitting on the couch together, she tells him, "You always know the right thing to say to me. I really thank God that he put you in my life. I am starting to really see and realize the importance of you being in my life. You have taught me so much in just a short amount of time with us being close friends," she says to him endearingly.

Craig says to her, "And know this. I will always be here for you whenever you need me."

They hug each other. Then she remembers that tomorrow is the wedding of Grace, and she asks him if he would join her there, but he lets her know he is in the wedding party already, and he lets her know that it will be a date for them.

They straighten and clean up the office from the late evening dinner date. Preparing to leave for the evening, she walks Craig to his car.

"Craig," she says, walking beside him.

"Yes, angel?" he says, giving her his undivided attention.

She thinks for a moment then shakes her head.

"It's nothing. Nothing, Craig," she says.

"You sure? It looked like it was really important, whatever you were getting ready to say," he says, facing her as they stop at his car.

"Nothing. I just wanted to thank you for coming out tonight and helping me get situated in my new office space. Please drive safely and call me when you make it home," she says, trying to hide her feelings.

He gets in to his car, telling her good night, and starts up the car and drives off. She walks back in the building, beating herself up mentally for not expressing her feelings, but she knows there is always next time.

The shift is over at the hospital, and she has got the office together enough to work in. Having taken care of everything in her office, she makes her way home to prepare for Grace's wedding, dreaming and wishing on the inside that it were her getting married instead, but the lingering thought continues in her head. *Be anxious for nothing. Because sometimes you get what you pray for.* Grace graciously had the dress delivered to the house. Rebecca pulls the bridesmaid party dress out of the bag, observing the delicate detail that was put into the dresses design. Standing in front of her mirror in her room, she drapes the dress over her and begins to think of Craig.

Rebecca turns as the phone rings, wondering who could be calling at this late hour. She picks up the phone and answers. "Hello?" she says with a question.

There is silence on the other end for a second; then he speaks, "Hey, angel," he says in soft, deep voice. A little smile comes across her face.

"Why aren't you in bed asleep?" she asks, still smiling.

"I am in bed. I was thinking about you and couldn't go to sleep. So I figured I'd take a chance and call you to see if you were still up. Why haven't you gone to bed yet?" he asks.

"Just trying to prepare ahead of time so I don't have to do any last-minute things for the wedding tomorrow because I know that Grace is going to need me," she says, sitting down in her chair in the sitting portion of the bedroom. "I am kind of excited. I haven't been to a formal affair in such a long time. It's nice to just dress up once in a while, socialize, and relax, forgetting about everything around you for a while, you know," she says.

"Yeah, I know where you're coming from. Since becoming a doctor, all I usually wind up going to are formal affairs or fundraisers for some medical event. But it will be nice to just relax amongst friends and not have to worry about someone asking for money, just being in your beautiful company."

She gets up from the chair with the phone on her ear and goes over to the dress on the bed and hangs it on the mirror and then goes into the bathroom, starting her shower water.

"Oh really? My beautiful company?"

"Yes," Craig says. "I was so glad to know that you were going to be coming to the wedding. I don't have to worry about being in bad company. We can dance until our feet get tired."

Rebecca is without words. She realizes she is being romanced, which feels good, instead of feeling like she is getting used or played.

"It feels good just to talk to someone without feeling like he is trying to take advantage of you," she says.

"Well, you know, angel, that is not what I am about. I am all about getting the will of God done, helping those that need it," Craig replies.

"Where are you at right now, Craig?" Rebecca asks.

"I am in bed, but it is so relaxing just talking to you," he replies.

"Well, not to cut you off, mister, but I am getting ready to get in my shower so I can at least get a little rest before the wedding tomorrow. I know it's going to be a very busy day," she says, changing from her clothes into her bathrobe. "I can't carry the phone into the shower, so I am going to bid you good night, noble sir. Close those dreamy eyes of yours and rest yourself, and I will see you later in the day," she says.

"Well, all right. I am turning over now. Good night, angel," he says.

"Good night, Craig," she says.

The night slowly passes as Rebecca anticipates sharing tomorrow with Craig. Something is definitely between them. Could this finally be the one for Rebecca? Could it be the promise of a future, and most of all, God's will being accomplished in both their lives? The morning finally breaks through the darkness of night like a flash of lightning breaking the sky into joyful rays of light everywhere. While she is lying in the middle of her bed, the alarm clock reaches the time of sound off. Today she doesn't have to worry about going into the hospital. This day is hers to enjoy and celebrate. She stretches her arms and legs in the bed and rolls over and looks at the picture of her son wrapped in the hospital blanket on her bedside. Sliding to the edge of the bed, she moves her neck around in a circular motion to pop it. Then gets up and goes into the bathroom and passes by the mirror and backs up and looks at her reflection. As she thinks of Craig, a smile breaks across her countenance. After finishing her shower, she comes out to the kitchen to prepare something to eat, knowing that this is going to be a long day for her being there for Grace on her wedding day.

As soon as she begins to prepare fruits and other items for breakfast, the phone rings. Scrambling to pick it up, she answers with excitement in her voice. "Good morning!"

"Well, good morning to you too, girl," Grace says, sounding cheerful as well.

"Oh, hey, Grace. How are you doing this morning?" she asks.

"Good. Sounds like you were expecting someone else to be on the other end," she says.

"Whatever, girl," Rebecca says, laughing.

"What are you doing right now?" Grace asks.

"I am doing my breakfast right now; then I will be headed your way, my dear," she says.

"Yeah, because you know that you guys got to get your hair and stuff done by the hairdresser and all the rest of the stuff that goes with it," Grace says.

"Don't worry. I got you, girl. I will be there in little bit. Don't stress yourself on your day. It is going to go perfectly, all right? I will see you in a few minutes, dear. Bye," she says.

Hanging up, she finishes eating breakfast. As she thinks about the little small details of the wedding that she is supposed to take care of, the phone rings again. Thinking that it is Grace again, she picks up the phone. "Yes, girl," she says.

"Good morning, angel. Is everything all right?" Craig says.

Her countenance changes immediately as she smiles.

"Good morning. How are you?" she says.

"I am doing great now I am talking to you. I really enjoyed our conversation last night. I slept like a baby after talking to you," he says. "I am looking forward to seeing you today."

"Oh, you are, Dr. Lowe?"

"Of course I am, Nurse Washington," he says, joking back with her. "So what time did you need me to pick you up?" Craig asks.

She responds in an apologetic tone. "I am so sorry, Craig. I just got a call from Grace. You know she is stressing over her big day, and she said she needed me. So I am going to go and meet with her and keep her under control and stress free, hopefully," she says, giggling.

"Well, then, angel, I guess I will see you there later. I guess I can do some things to help Daryl today as well. You know, all I am trying to do really is see your face," Craig responds, being serious.

Rebecca starts giggling again on the phone at his compliment. "I hate to get off the phone with you, but I have to get myself together and get out of this house before I get in trouble with Grace. I will see you later.".

"All right. See you later, boo," he replies.

They hang up the phone, and she finishes up her food quickly, straightens up the kitchen, and runs in the bedroom to get all the stuff she has set aside for the day.

A half hour has passed by; she makes it to the country club. She finds Grace up in the prep room getting her hair fixed for her veil to fit. Rebecca walks into the room. "Hey, girl. I am here now. I took care of some of the small things for you, as requested. The wedding cake is on the way here to be set up for you. I checked with your wedding coordinator; everything is running smoothly, honey," Rebecca says, checking off things on her to-do list.

Grace sits in the styling chair while the stylist continues to work on her hair. Rebecca walks over to her and looks at her. "How are you holding up, hon?"

"I am doing the best I can. I just want this day to be as perfect as possible. I am glad that you are here now, Becky," she says, wiggling her hands.

"Don't worry; everything will be great. They say there is always a little stress and apprehension. But it always turns out great. Just relax and let things roll along; go with the flow. It's not going to help you worrying about everything. Enjoy your day. Nothing can ruin this. You are marrying the man you love, right?" Rebecca says.

Grace nods her head in agreement and lets out a big exhale.

Grace opens her eyes and thanks Rebecca and says, "Girl, you are just positively glowing today and seem to know the right thing to say. What's got you glowing?"

Rebecca starts smiling and grinning. "Am I glowing? I tell you it must be the God up above. He is doing great things for me. But this day is not about me. You've devoted a lot of time getting me together; it's all about you today, my friend," she says, still grinning.

"I see you don't want to share. Is that what it is?" Grace asks, sitting back in the chair and smiling.

"I just feel really good inside, like I am healed. Like God just did an operation on the inside of my soul and heart, just repaired me" she says, shaking her head and smiling.

"It is good to see you so positive and sure of yourself. It's a side of you I have rarely seen," Grace says proudly. As Grace gets up out of the chair from getting her hair done, she goes over to the table for her nails to get done. Rebecca sits in the chair to get her hair styled, but she continues to explain her statement.

"To finally meet someone who really cares about me is just mind boggling to me. This friendship has helped me see that it's not all about the physical aspect of love but the love of the soul, being there for the ups and downs of a person," she says.

Grace looks at her. "Girl, what have you got tied up in, or should I say who?" she says, giggling.

Rebecca pauses, looking around the room, which is filled with Grace's family and a few friends from the hospital.

"It's like God just steered me to this person. He has such spiritual insight that I had never seen before, especially for a doctor. He is unlike any other man I have met, almost like an angel sent from God."

Grace's mouth drops open, and then she smiles. "Oh my God. I can't believe it. You two have hooked up finally?" she says, getting excited.

"No, we are just good friends, even though I would like it to be more," Rebecca says.

All the women in the room are looking and start saying, "Well, who is this wonderful man?"

"I am sorry, ladies. I am not giving a name. You know how gossip always starts, and we are really good friends. I don't want to mess that up," she says.

The stylist starts working on her hair, and Rebecca crosses her legs, sitting back. Grace is without words.

"I told you, girl. I don't want this day to be about me," Rebecca says. "I know that your mother already has something old for you, but I have something borrowed for you, girl."

Grabbing her bag right by the chair, she pulls out a rectangular case. Rebecca hands it to one of Grace's sister's to give it to her. Opening the case, Grace begins to cry and says, "I can't believe it. Your favorite emerald and diamond bracelet. Thank you so much," Grace says, tearing up.

The room is filled with an overwhelming thickness of emotions dealing with the wedding, friendship, and the bonds of love that tie them all together to celebrate a day of love between two individuals who plan to spend the rest of their lives together.

After all the festivities going on in the changing room with the women, the time has passed on, and the women are now ready for the ceremony, most of all, the bride to be. Rebecca has done a good job of keeping things together for Grace, making sure that all things have gone according to Grace's expectations. Grace stands in front of the mirror, waiting until it is time for her to march down the aisle. Rebecca stands there before she has to march and tells her how proud she is of her and the man that she has found for her life, wishing her all the blessings that the Lord can give them. Then Rebecca comes at the wedding coordinator's signal to march down the stairs to meet her escort. Having coordinated the way they are supposed to move and march, she meets her escort down at the bottom of the steps. Putting her hand out in order for the escort to take it, it's no coincidence that Craig would be her escort for the wedding party. You can see the obvious chemistry between both of them when they walk down the aisle up to the altar. They continue to look at each other and grin while they march until they reach their stopping point at the altar.

Making it to the stopping point, they part to their own sides. They continue to look at each other and smile, even as the other bridal party marches and places themselves in their positions for the ceremony. Then the wedding march music starts playing for the bride. All eyes are on the bride as she comes down the steps, dressed in her delicately beaded white dress and long train. Finally, the bride reaches the destination of the preacher and her mate. She is taken by the man she plans to pledge and entrust her life and love to. The wedding vows are completed with the preacher's empowerment of joining as man and wife. They salute each other with a kiss full of passion. Craig and Rebecca look at each other as the newly married couple kisses. The married couple turns around to the audience, and the preacher announces them as Mr. and Mrs. Miller. Everyone claps. And the wedding party departs back down to the aisle to begin the reception at the country club.

There is so much going on with the wedding party trying to get all the pictures before they sit down for the dinner. It's so busy that Craig and Rebecca haven't been able to talk. An hour and thirty minutes have passed, and all the pictures have been taken care of, and the wedding party has been seated in their proper places at the wedding party table. Different announcements have been made by the wedding coordinator, ensuring that everything is going in order and time sequence according to the wishes of the bride. Craig whispers to Rebecca in her ear, and she giggles and grins. The groom makes a toast to his wife, and then Craig stands up as the groom takes his seat and gives a toast to the bride and the groom. The country club gets quiet.

"You know, at first when I was going through my life, I didn't think marriage was really possible, but I see it now in my own life. I have seen it in my friend and his lovely bride, Grace, who have been nothing but an example of true love. They have a union created by God himself, something that will last forever with all the blessings, love, and passion that goes with it. Daryl and Grace, may the blessings of the Lord be upon your marriage, along with all the happiness that you both can take. I love you both," he says, raising his glass. He looks at Rebecca, and she just smiles at him.

When the formalities of the wedding celebration are over, they are free to go down and get on the dance floor. The bride and groom are the first on the floor. It is dark outside the country club. Although it's dark outside, it is lit up with decorations of white lights.

Craig and Rebecca are still at the wedding table talking. Then he puts out his hand and asks her if she wouldn't mind dancing with him. She begins to blush a little then replies to him, "It would be my pleasure, sir," taking his hand as he leads her to the dance floor. Then he turns around quickly and grabs her waist and pulls her close to him, and they dance together as one to the slow jam playing in the background of the country club reception hall. The floor is crowded with everyone having a good time celebrating, but to them it's like they are the only ones; they're engulfed in each other's presence.

"You know, I am really glad that we were able to have an outing like this together, even if it is a wedding party," Craig says in her ear.

Rebecca takes her head from off his chest and looks up at him. "Why do you say that, Craig?" she says coyly.

He pauses and looks deep into her eyes and leads her out on the veranda of the country club. She looks at him with uncertainty, but his look puts her at ease.

They find a cozy spot outside to talk privately.

"There just hasn't been enough time to share with you what I always wanted to. Having lunch and sitting down together and talking, it just never seems to be the right time or the conversation, just never led into the direction I wanted in order to be able to ask you," he says, standing in front of her.

She looks up at him again intensely and asks him, "What?" with butterflies in her stomach, only hoping that it isn't another devastating blow to her life since he has been such a rock.

"I want you to know you have been nothing but a jewel to me that I have found," he says.

Breaking the eye contact, she looks down, holding her drink in her hand and preparing herself for whatever the news is, expecting the worst. He stretches forth his hand and lifts her face to look at him.

"Fret not, my angel. It isn't what you think," he says.

She can feel her legs getting weak, as if they are going to collapse out from under her, so she has a seat on the stone bench behind her. Then he kneels down in front of her and puts his hand on her knee and bows his head for a split second and takes a swallow, along with a breath, and begins to talk again.

"I believe ... no, I know that I have found just the one that I have been looking for all my life, who fits perfectly in everything that I do, and I don't want to lose that. I believe and know that special someone is you, angel. I have been praying and seeking the Lord continually when it came to our relationship. I knew God had placed me in your life for a reason. Even though things got a little rough during times, the Lord just told me to be there no matter what and continue to stand still and wait. I feel that you are my best friend, someone I can be myself with, that perfect fit. That rib I can share everything with. What I am trying to say, angel, is that I love you with all my heart, my soul, my mind, with everything that I am. I love you," he says, being heartfelt.

Rebecca's mouth drops open. Things around her get tuned out and hazy with no words, but tears roll down her cheeks. She sets her wine glass to the side as Craig takes both of her hands.

"I hope that you feel the same way that I do," he says.

All she can do at this moment is nod her head for yes, trembling and speechless.

"I would love it if you would do me the great honor of sharing your life with me and becoming my wife," he says.

Everything within her drops; she can't believe what is happening. "I am sorry, Craig. Can you repeat that last part?" she says, looking dazed.

He smiles at her with a crooked smile and pulls the ring out of his pocket while he is down on his knee and says again, "Would you do me the honor, my beautiful angel, of becoming my wife?"

She looks at the ring and looks at him with her hand over her mouth and tears flowing, thinking, *It can't get any better than this.*

"Um, angel, it requires a response," he says, smiling.

Coming to herself, she says, "Yes. Yes, yes, yes, yes. I would love to be your wife, Craig. Love to."

She puts her hand out for him to put the ring on her finger; he places it on her finger, and she places her hands on his face, pulling him to her, and she kisses him deeply. Automatically, he embraces her by putting his arms around her. Pulling back, she looks at him.

"Do you really want to be with me? With all my drama and things I have gone through?" she says, still in unbelief.

He laughs and puts his head down again for a second. "You're kidding, right? Of course I do. I love everything about you, angel," he says, reassuring her.

She embraces him and kisses him on his lips quickly. Another song comes on. "Aw, that's my song," Rebecca says with her hand in the air moving around, and she grabs his hand, running back into the country club. On the dance floor, Rebecca can't stop smiling, looking into Craig's eyes; then the bride, Grace, walks over to them both while they are dancing and laughing.

"Well, it looks like the two of you are having a great time," Grace says, overjoyed.

"Grace, the wedding was awesome, girl, and the reception is even better. You look perfect, girl," Rebecca says, still holding on to Craig.

While Rebecca's hands go down his arms, Grace notices the rock on her finger.

"Oh my God! Is that what I think it is, girl?" Grace says with her eyes bulging, grabbing her hand, looking at the ring, and then looking at Rebecca again.

"Yes, it is, girl," she responds, moving her neck and head and laughing.

Grace pulls her from Craig and screams with excitement, jumping up and down.

"Oh my God," Grace says again. "I am so hyped about this and at my reception of all places."

Everybody kind of looks at them while they are leaping up and down; then Grace runs over to the microphone, calling everybody's attention to Craig and Rebecca, announcing their engagement. They both look at each other, holding each other's hands.

"This is quite a surprise. These two come full circle because, of course, I tried to set them up and that didn't work in the beginning, but it's wonderful to know now they are engaged and on the day of my wedding," she says.

She gets a glass of wine and raises it, saying, "Everybody, a toast to the future Mr. and Mrs. Craig Lowe. God's blessing and love shower down on you both forever. I love you both." After everyone drinks to the toast, they clap in celebration of their engagement, continuing the party.

eleven

Nine months after the engagement of Rebecca and Craig, things are going pretty well as they plan the wedding details with only two months until the event of their nuptials. They are in one of the department stores in the mall, scanning items for their wedding registry, laughing at the different things they pick out. Someone happens to walk up to them as they are talking to each other.

"Hello, Bee," the person says. She turns around.

"Oh, hello, Philip," she says awkwardly.

"Dr. Craig Lowe, this is Minister Philip McNair. Minister McNair, this is my fiancé, Dr. Craig Lowe," she says proudly.

Craig reaches out to shake Philip's hand. He can see that Philip is kind of hesitant, hearing that he is her fiancé. Then Minister McNair's wife pulls on him to introduce her, but Rebecca interrupts him.

"We've met, remember? I already know her. If you'll excuse us, we have to finish scanning things for our wedding registry," Rebecca says rudely.

"It was nice to have met you both," Craig says.

They begin to walk off from Philip and his wife; then Philip walks up to them and, excusing himself, asks Craig if he could speak to Rebecca for a second. He looks at Rebecca, and she looks at him.

"If she wants to talk to you, I am okay with it," he says calmly, looking at Rebecca and nodding to her. "Go ahead, angel."

Philip pulls her to the side for a second, looking back at his wife and Craig; then Rebecca quickly speaks with her arms folded. "What is it that you have to say to me, Philip, that you couldn't have said a long time ago?" she says, looking at him with disgust. "You've caused me a lot of heartache and pain."

Philip has his head down as she talks. "I know I did, and I wanted to apologize for the wrong that Tanya and I did to you."

"Why? Why now would you apologize when you had so many months to do that?" Rebecca says with a chilly tone.

Then Craig walks over to her and puts his hand on each side of her arms. "Angel," he says.

"I am all right, baby. I'll be there in a second," she says, looking back at him.

Then Philip looks at both of them, glances at his wife, and then looks back. "I am so sorry for what we did to you and your son. I figured if I ever saw you again that I would do right and apologize for my cruelness. I believe that is why the Lord has not allowed us to have children. My wife had a horrible miscarriage, and now the doctors say we can't have children.

So I am standing here now, saying to you we are so very sorry for our actions," he says. Turning around, he takes his wife's hand, and they walk off.

Rebecca rolls her eyes and shakes her head. Craig nudges Rebecca and whispers in her ear, "Angel, forgive and let it go; don't hold on to that anymore."

Looking up into his brown eyes, she closes her eyes, puts her head down, and shakes her head. Then tears start to fall. He bends his knees slightly to look into her face.

"Angel, what is wrong?"

"It's nothing. Just seeing him today made all those memories rush back about Aaron," she says with her arms still crossed and hand up by her nose.

Craig stands there, embracing her. "That's all right, baby. I am here for you."

She embraces him as well. "You want to go home? We can do this some other day."

She shakes her head no. "I'm all right, babe. I'm not going to let my past affect me."

Though seeing Philip and his wife brought back painful memories, she was able to cope with the help of the Almighty and the presence of her man.

Rebecca stands there for a second. When she begins to think to herself, she feels sorry for the couple's plight. She thinks of all the bad things that Philip did and how his wife has to pay for what transpired. *You reap what you sow.* Craig comes back over to her and gently rubs her on her back. "You all right, angel? Pain and stress are hard to process sometimes. But I do want to tell you I am proud of the way that you handled the situation. God has really begun a new work in you."

As he hugs her from behind, she smiles, coming back to the matter at hand, planning and picking out stuff for their wedding registry. Continuing on through the store, she reflects on what Craig has says to her, thinking of how she has changed, how the Lord has shown himself to her little by little in her life, especially through this man that has been given to her. While he is talking, she just looks at him, not believing the blessing that she has been given.

"What is it?" he says, smirking.

"Nothing," she says and then pauses. "I am just thanking God for you. I almost messed up some things, trying to do them my way, doing my own thing to ensure I was happy," she says, squeezing his arm as she holds onto him and lays her head on his shoulder.

"I wasn't going anywhere as long as the Lord told me to stick around, especially for a beautiful and graceful lady as yourself. I didn't want to miss out on what he had for me."

Rebecca looks at him, overwhelmed by his talk of how wonderful and graceful she is.

"You know, sweetie, sometimes I think that you are just a dream come true."

Craig looks at her and chuckles. She looks at him with a little frown on her face at the fact that he is laughing at her while she is trying to express herself to him.

"Oh, angel, don't take offense at my laughter. It's not at you; it is at myself. For one thing, I am not perfect, as you will see when we are married and living with each other. That is when the real test comes. You really get to see the other side of the ones you love. I feel the same for you. I believe that you are a dream come true for me. I see a lot of greatness in you, angel, that you don't see. I feel that we balance each other."

"You really feel that way about me?"

"Of course I do, angel. I love you. Not just the love that everybody speaks of. I love you with the love that God gave me for you, the love like Christ had for the church that he gave his life for it. I would do the same for you, my love," he says.

The words Craig spoke take her very breath away. Tears begin to fill her eyes as she fans her face and smiles, looking at him and continuing to fall more in love with the God that is inside of him.

The hours have passed within the day. They have completed the things on their agenda. Craig drops her back off at home. The phone rings, and she lets the answering machine pick up. Then she hears her mother's voice. She quickly picks up the phone.

"What's up, Momma?" she says, kind of out of breath.

"Is something wrong? Your voice sounds a little funny. Is everything all right?" Mother asks.

"I am all right. Just happy, that's all," she says.

Mom Washington pauses for a second, "I was lying before the Lord today, and God showed me your face. He spoke to me restoration for you. Double shall your blessing be; what was lost to you shall be restored to you double, says the Lord. I didn't call for anything else except tell you just that. I love you, baby," she says, hanging up the phone.

Rebecca is left in a state of amazement as she tries to figure out what her mother is talking about. She sits down in the family room of the house with nothing but silence surrounding her. Her mind begins to race back through various different things in her life. After a few minutes, her head begins to ache. Then she comes to herself, *Girl, rest your mind, and stop trying to figure out what God is going to do in your life.*

A little while later, the phone rings.

"Hello?" she says in a soft tone.

A deep voice that she doesn't recognize says, "Hey, how are you doing?"

"All right, and who, may I ask, is speaking?"

"It's Jacob."

Something clicks in her. "I thought I asked you not to call me anymore. That we're done. There was no reason for us to stay in contact after Aaron's death," she says.

"Come on, Rebecca. Please don't be that way. I really need someone to talk to right now," Jacob pleads.

Rebecca stands there with her head to the side and her lips pursed, feeling knots in her stomach. "Why call me, Jacob? Why not call your other women that you have?" she says coldly.

There is silence on his end for a few seconds.

"I really felt there was no other person I could talk to but you because you would know how I feel."

"What do you mean that I would know how you feel? I gave up a long time ago trying to figure out how you feel and how I could make you feel," she says coldly.

He responds with a sorrowful voice, "That's what I wanted to talk to you about. I feel so empty. I could have had everything with you, Rebecca, and I did you so wrong. I blew it, especially when it came down to our son. I feel so empty without him in my life. Don't you?"

The mention of Aaron stirs her emotions within her. She closes her eyes.

"Yes, of course I miss him. I miss him every minute, every second of the day. I deal with it every day, Jacob, but I've learned that I have to move on with my life, and so should you. I blamed you and blamed others for what happened to my Aaron, but I realized with the help of God and my man that some things, even bad things, happen for a reason, and we learn to live with the scars of those events, be healed, and move to the next level in our lives and learn how to be happy," she explains.

. "How can you move on and cut me off and act like you and I and our son never happened?" he asks.

"What do you mean cut you off? If you're looking for a confrontation, Jacob, I can't give that to you. I don't have that left in me. I wouldn't be true to myself if I tried to act like you weren't a part of my life at one time or like my son didn't happen. I carried him. I loved him growing inside of me for almost seven months. He is a part of me and will always be. And as far as you and me, the old Rebecca would have done anything to keep you, no matter how bad you treated me, due to the way I felt about myself. Since then I have experienced a love that has shown me that I am worth more than a one-night stand. I am worth more than just the skin I am in. I am a treasure to my man, and most of all, to God," she says.

"So what? You're telling me now that you have someone in your life?"

Rebecca picks up that he is still trying to find a reason to argue and debate with her. She takes a moment, feeling her heart pounding in her chest, but she finds the strength to calm the anger brewing.

"Hello? Are you still there?"

"Yes, Jacob, I am still here. You know one thing that I am learning now is how to forgive, no matter how a person may come off, and the first thing I had to do was forgive myself. That is what leads to the road for healing. What I had to do also is forgive those around me. So that is what I am going to do for you. I forgive you, Jacob, and I want you to forgive me for being mean and cold hearted toward you when both of us were hurting due to our loss, but now we both can continue our lives. Believe me; I understand that you are hurting right now from not having our son, but nothing will bring him back. Forgive yourself, man, and find some meaning and purpose for your life," she says.

"Well, I feel better now that I have been able to release something else in my life that was a burden. Thank you, Jacob. You have helped me more than you know in this conversation we have shared, but now I will ask you this one last time, not being mean or facetious, please don't call my house anymore. This chapter of my life and yours is now and will forever be closed, never to open again. Good-bye, Jacob."

A moment later, Jacobs says, "All right, Rebecca. Good-bye."

Hanging the phone up, she says, "Yes!" She brings her knee up and her elbow down as a sign of victory, knowing that this battle with past obstacles and issues is over, feeling the weight of the excess baggage in her life lift off her. She bends her head back and just smiles, happy that she was able to deal successfully with conflicts and get victory without getting flustered and bent out of shape.

She heads to her bedroom, and the phone rings again. She glances at the time, seeing that the hour is late. Hesitating to pick up the phone for fear that it might be Jacob again, she goes over to look at the caller ID on the phone on her nightstand before the answering machine picks up. Recognizing the number, she smiles and presses the talk button on the phone. "Hey, babe," she says.

"Hey, angel. How are you doing?"

"I am doing all right now that I am hearing your voice," she replies.

"I was trying to call you, but the phone was busy; then I called back, and it was just ringing. I got a little worried," he says.

She pauses before she speaks, trying to think of how she can tell him whom she was talking with. "I do apologize. I heard the line beeping, but I was talking with Jacob," she says.

He pauses for a second or two. "What was he calling you for?"

Sensing the tension in his voice, she smiles, feeling that he is a little jealous and uneasy about whom she has just conversed with. "Relax, my love. It was nothing, nothing you should be upset or concerned about," she says sweetly.

"Shouldn't I be, knowing that he is calling you? Not that I don't trust you. I just know him from everything you have shared with me," he says, with his voice uneasy.

"Well, sounds like you're a little jealous to me," she says with snicker.

"Yeah I am, I must admit. I'm not going to even try to hide it," he says, sounding ashamed.

She laughs. "That's all right. I am flattered that you would get like that, lets me know that you're still interested in me," she says.

"What are you doing right now?" he asks.

"I am getting ready to take my shower so I can prepare for work tomorrow," she says. "Getting back to the subject of Jacob because you know I want to share everything with you, no secrets. I don't know really why he called, but I think it was God helping me to move on in life and to love you without limits and baggage. He was trying to find out why I cut him off, besides the obvious of losing Aaron. I let him know now that I have a man that has taught me things I never knew or never tried to know," she explains.

"It wasn't difficult for you to talk to him about that?" he asks.

"I was quite surprised at myself. The things that came out of my mouth were so different than how I would have handled it if I had not had any help or healing," she says.

"Is that so?" he says humorously.

"You know, it's all because of this fantastic man that the Lord gave me who allowed himself to be used. I really thank you for all of what you done for me. Thank you," she says.

"So, really, it was closing another chapter pretty much again," Craig says.

She agrees with a little laugh. "It's amazing to me how all this happened in a short amount of time with coming in contact with these men in one day. After so many months of pain and issues, I am able to put them behind me with the Lord's help."

"That is amazing that in a short time you were able to overcome and forgive no matter what happened to you in the past with these dudes. You are really growing, angel. I am really proud of you. Words can't even explain how I feel. Oh, I also wanted to find out if you wanted to have lunch with Daryl and your girl tomorrow."

"Yeah, that would be cool. I don't think it should get too busy for me tomorrow. I am getting in the shower. I love you and miss you. I will see you tomorrow, all right, boo? Bye-bye."

He bids her a good night.

• • •

The next morning Rebecca awakes energized. She stands up, stretching, and then bends to get her digital planner, checking to see what all she has to do today for work and the wedding. She remembers the conversation she had with Craig last night about the lunch date with Grace and Daryl, adding that in on her digital planner. Beginning the day with her normal routine, she changes things up by having a short devotional prayer before she leaves the house, something she hasn't really done before. With her eyes closed, she silently asks the Lord to be with her throughout the day.

A little later, she pulls up in the parking lot. Her cell phone rings.

"Hello?" she answers.

"Hey, sweetie. I am glad that I caught you. How are you doing this morning?" Mom Washington asks.

"I am doing good this morning. Running just a little slow, kind of tired, that's all," she responds.

"Your father and I were wondering if you and Craig would be able to make it to a dinner tonight at our house, kind of a family get-together," Mom asks.

"Well, I will have to check with Craig to see if that is okay with him because we already have a lunch date scheduled with another couple. So if it is all right with you, Momma, I will call you back and let you know," she says, grabbing her bag from the backseat of the truck and walking quickly into the building, her black squared pumps beating the pavement with quick steps with her bell-bottom pants and blue silk blouse blowing in the wind. "All right, Momma. I have to go into the building now. I will call you back, okay?" she says.

"You know, your father would love to see you guys tonight. Having the whole family there would mean a lot to us, Becca."

Rebecca doesn't say anything, feeling as though Mom Washington is trying to lay a guilt trip on her. "Okay, Momma. I told you I will have to give you a call back to make sure it is all right for him to make it. Okay, bye, Momma," she says again.

Mom Washington acknowledges and hangs up.

Rebecca notices the lobby of the hospital seems a little busy as she maneuvers her way through the lobby to the elevator. Looking down the corridor that leads to Craig's office, she thinks about stopping in to see if he has made it to work yet, but she continues to make her way to her office. There is not really that much activity going on in the burn unit today. Lying her bag on her couch in the office, she walks over to check to see if there are any messages on her phone.

Slowly making her way over to the mirror in her office, she listens to the message, hearing that Dr. Raymond Reynolds has left her a message asking her to meet with him in thirty minutes to discuss business of importance. *What could this business of importance be?* she thought. The answering machine completes the message, and she pulls her hair into a bun. *I feel like I am about to go on a first date. I am so nervous.* Quickly going over to her desk, she calls Craig's cell phone to see where he is.

"Hello, angel. It is good to hear your voice this morning."

She smiles while she sits at the desk. "It is good to

hear my man's voice too this morning. You sound so good," she replies. "I was calling you to let you know just in case you tried to call or something, I have to go into a meeting in less than thirty minutes with Dr. Reynolds."

"Why do you have to go see him?"

"I don't know. Hopefully they are not looking to move me again. You know how they like to move the nurses around in the hospital," she comments.

"Yeah, I know. You wouldn't have to worry about that, my love, if you would go back to school and become a full-fledged MD," Craig suggests.

"Yeah, I know, but I was also calling you because I got a call from my mother. She would like us to have dinner with them tonight, but I told her that I have to check with you to see what your schedule was like," she says.

"That's soon."

Rebecca, still sitting in the chair at the desk, scanning her planner for the day, comments, "Is that something that you will be able to do if your schedule is not too crazy?"

"Angel, you know I would move heaven and earth if I could just to be near you."

He reminds her of their lunch date with Daryl and Grace in the afternoon and tells her that he has to get off the phone and he will get with her later. Rebecca, sitting in her office with her head back on the chair, looks at her watch and jumps up to rush to Dr. Reynolds's office for the meeting he has set. Rebecca racks her brain, trying to figure out what the meeting is all about. Taking a breath, she walks down the corridor. She finally makes it to the office of Dr. Reynolds. She puts her hands on her hips and bows her head for a second, taking a deep breath, and raises it back up, using her hand to move her hair out of her face. She puts her hand on the door and knocks and opens the door after hearing him say come in.

"Good morning, Dr. Reynolds. You wanted to see me for a meeting, sir?" she asks nervously. She walks into the office, seeing him standing by the window with the morning rays of the sun brightening up the office. "I sure did, Nurse Washington," he says as he walked toward her. "Please have a seat."

He directs her toward the chairs in front of his desk. Sitting down, she crosses her legs. Dr. Reynolds has a seat in his leather chair.

"I called you in the office today, Ms. Washington, to let you know that we have been viewing your work for quite some time here throughout the hospital in the various units that you have been in," Dr. Reynolds says with his hands together at the fingertips, looking directly in her eyes, not breaking contact.

He continues the conversation after a pause. "I must say your work does speak for itself and your level of customer service and caring that you give to each patient is second to none. We want to make an investment in you."

Her mouth drops open in astonishment. She had thought in the beginning that she might get laid off or cut back in hours.

"What type of investment are you talking about, sir?"

"I know that a lot of nurses don't usually transition over to the side of being a medical doctor, but hearing the input of surrounding doctors and seeing some of your work firsthand shows your ability to be a doctor," he says, pausing. "So what do you think?

With her mind running fifty miles a minute, thinking of all the work that she would have to do in becoming a doctor, the money that she would have to pay, and the time that it would put in, it begins to overwhelm her.

Immediately, she says, "I am sorry, Dr. Reynolds. I don't think I would be able to do that right now. The time and money that it would take would just be too much for me right now."

"I guess you didn't hear me, Nurse Washington. We are willing to invest in you as long as you come back to this hospital to do residency and continue to work in the burn unit. This means we are willing to fund all of this for you. We have a new program within the confines of this hospital, a program I have been trying to push for quite some time now. Every four years, we pick an outstanding and deserving nurse who is set apart from the rest and offer him or her this opportunity," he explains.

She sits there speechless on what has just been offered to her on a silver platter. "I can't believe it. Dr. Reynolds, is this a joke?" she says, finally after the shock of the news.

Dr. Reynolds just smiles at her. "No, dear. This is

a real proposition and opportunity for you if you want to take it," he says as he leans back in his chair again with his elbows on the armrests.

Standing up from the chair, she leaps up and down. "Yes, yes, I will take this opportunity. Thank you," she says, running over to him. He stands up, and she hugs him, thanking him again.

"It wasn't just me that made the decision. It was a board of doctors who thought you would be a good candidate for this. Congratulations to you; you deserve this chance," he says, shaking her hand.

After that, she turns around and leaves the office, tearing at the opportunity that has come her way. Finally exiting Dr. Reynolds's office, she closes the door and then leans back on it, looking up to the heavens with a smile on her face.

Rebecca begins to walk down the hallway from his office with her hands in her pocket to keep from clapping them. She begins to laugh within herself. *I can't wait to tell Craig about this.* Pulling herself together from the excitement from the news, she prepares to go back to the office and see the patients on the appointment log. Making it back to the burn unit, she pauses outside before she enters the room with a patient in it, still thanking God for this new unseen blessing coming into her life.

twelve

Rebecca takes a seat after her rounds throughout the unit. She ponders over everything that is falling into place. While sitting at the desk, looking through different items, she remembers the lunch date. She grabs her keys and bag and then rushes out of the door, praying and hoping that she will not be late, knowing the time it will take to get to the restaurant chosen for the lunch date. Making it to her truck, she gets a call from Paige.

"Hey, sista, what's up?" Paige says.

"I am on my way out to a lunch date with Craig and a few friends. Did you need something, sista?" Rebecca asks.

"I was calling you to find out if you can bring something to the get-together tonight, preferably a dessert," Paige requests.

"Yeah, sure I can do that. I got to go now, sweetie. I will talk to you later, okay?" she says, hanging up the phone.

Finally making it to the J. Alexander Restaurant

from the Memphis lunchtime traffic, she gets out of the truck, quickstepping into the restaurant. She dashes to the restroom to change out the hospital uniform into something more presentable. She can already see that the lunch party has arrived and has been seated. While she is in the restroom, she pulls out a little wraparound brown dress out of her bag, and her cell phone rings again. "Yes, babe?" she answers.

"Where are you?" Craig says, sounding a little agitated.

"I'm here, sweetie. I'm coming out of the stall in the restroom," she says, checking herself in the mirror with the earpiece on, fixing and pulling on the dress. "I'm almost finished. I will be out in a minute. My meeting ran a little late with Dr. Reynolds."

"All right. I will see you in a minute," he says, hanging up.

When Rebecca turns the corner coming out of the restroom, heading toward the table, Craig sees her and stands up, smiling as she comes toward him.

"Hey, everybody!" she says cheerfully, coming around the table to greet Craig first.

"Hey, baby," he says, kissing her on the cheek.

"I apologize for my lateness. I didn't expect for the meeting with Dr. Reynolds to last as long as it did," she says.

Craig pulls out her chair for her to sit down and puts the napkin in her lap. Craig leans down and kisses her on the cheek again.

"Aww, isn't that precious?" Grace says.

"Man, this is crazy to me," Daryl says, sitting back

in the chair, leaning to the side where Grace is. Grace looks at him with her elbow on the table and her hand on her head, asking, "What do you mean?"

He has everyone's attention. "You know, with us all knowing each other, Grace and I being married. Now you guys are getting married. It just seems so ironic," Daryl says, chuckling.

"You know it took an arm, a leg, and a prayer for me to get this girl to even come on a blind date to meet you, even after seeing you almost every day at the hospital," Grace comments.

Rebecca laughs, hanging her head in shame. Craig leans over to her and whispers in her ear, "You don't have to be ashamed of anything because you got what God wanted you to have in the end."

She giggles with her chin to her chest, turning her head to look at him.

"What are you two talking about over there? Are you going to share?" Grace comments with her finger underneath her chin.

"Uh, no. It's between me and my man," she says, laughing.

"Okay. Okay, I see. Ain't nothing wrong with that," Grace replies.

Rebecca begins to reminisce. "You know, I still remember when Grace got me to come on the blind date, not knowing that I would be meeting the man that I am going to marry, the man that God blessed me with," she says proudly to all of them. "I am glad now, though, especially that he had patience with me and didn't give up on pursuing me, making me feel wanted and loved."

Craig puts his hand on her back, rubbing her lovingly; then he stands up to give a toast to both couples, saying a few words and is interrupted by his name being called. "Craig?" a female voice calls. "Craig, is that you? Oh my God. I can't believe it!" the female voice continues. And silence falls over the oval table where they are sitting. Rebecca turns and looks to see who this woman is calling his name. Then she looks at Craig and then gives looks to Daryl and Grace to see if they knew who the young lady is. Daryl puts his head down.

"Oh my Lord," Craig says under his breath, still holding his refreshment in the air for the toast. The woman comes up and hugs him.

"I can't believe it is you, Craig. What a shock to run into you here," the woman said.

"Jennifer, what are you doing here in Tennessee?" he asks.

Rebecca continues to look on with concern. Craig has a worried look on his face.

"Hey, Daryl. How are you doing? My job transferred me down here to get some stuff in order. You know how it is," she says, giggling and flirting with her hand still on Craig's arm.

Grace looks at Daryl. He shakes his head and whispers to her, "That is Craig's old girl. I didn't have anything to do with her."

Rebecca clears her throat to get his attention.

"I am sorry, Jennifer, this is my angel, Rebecca, my fiancé," he says, placing his hand on her shoulder.

Rebecca stands to shake Jennifer's hand. "Hello, Jennifer, pleased to meet you," she says in her professional tone.

"Oh, somebody finally gotcha, huh? Finally got him to commit? Ain't you a lucky one, honey?" Jennifer says jokingly with her flirtatious laugh.

"And exactly how do you know Craig?" Rebecca asks, watching Jennifer eyeball Craig with her hand on her hip.

"We knew each other back in Illinois some time ago," she says with a smile on her face, putting her hand on his arm again, leaning into him.

"Oh, you did, huh?" Rebecca says, her jealous side starting to show.

"Well, I do apologize for interrupting, but I have to get to my lunch date. Busy day, you know how it is. Ta-ta," Jennifer says and then walks off.

Craig sits down and looks at Rebecca out of the corner of his eye. She smiles with her lips closed tightly together, shaking her head and begins eating her meal.

"You good, angel?" Craig asks with a worried look on his face.

Grace and Daryl just look on. Grace, feeling the tension from Rebecca, tries to change the conversation and go in another direction, but it doesn't work. After that, the lunch begins to go sour. Everyone finishes their lunches in silence. Rebecca rises up from her seat from the table and hugs Daryl and Grace, telling them good-bye. She turns to Craig, coldly telling him to have a good day.

Craig stands there. Grace looks at Craig in disbelief. Rebecca leaves.

Rebecca is all bent out of shape. She looks at the door for Craig to come running out after her, but of course that doesn't happen, which fuels the fire for her even more. She gets in her truck and speeds back to work with all kinds of thoughts racing through her mind. *Could I have made another mistake with this man? He says he loves me but didn't even come after me.* All these crazy thoughts continue to run on through her head. Finally making it back to the hospital, she goes into the bathroom and cries a little, wiping her eyes and straightening herself after changing back into her nurse's uniform.

By evening time, Rebecca has finished her duties. Getting her paperwork and books together, she begins to walk to the door. Craig walks in the office. Rebecca is completely caught off guard at his showing up. He sighs and begins to talk, but she cuts him off. "I don't want to hear it, Craig," she says. She tries to walk around him, out of the office, but he quickly blocks the way out, stopping her from exiting.

"You're not getting off that easy. I don't even think so," Craig says.

"What do you mean me getting off easy? Aren't you the one with the extra girlfriend?" she says angrily.

"Come on, angel. You know it is not like that. I never said that I didn't have a past, but that is just what it is, the past. I am sure we are not finished seeing or dealing with stuff from my past and your past, but we can't let the past rule our lives and dictate to us what our futures will be.

"I am not like the men you've dealt with in the past. I told you I have a past too. It's not a messy one, but it is a past. I admit I am not perfect; nobody is but Christ. I am here, and I am willing and ready to take the ride with you in our lives and invest in you. Aren't you? No matter the cost?"

"You didn't even come after me when I left the restaurant or at least try to explain," she says.

Craig pauses and looks at her. "Explain to you about what, angel? Something that has been dead and dormant for years?" he says.

Rebecca doesn't say a word and starts to walk out the door, and Craig begins to walk behind her.

"So, what? Is that it now? Are you giving up on me? Giving up on us?" Craig asks.

She turns around swiftly with an angry look on her face. "I didn't say that, did I?"

"No."

"Then why would you say that?"

Craig takes her by her arm and keeps her from walking farther.

"The reason I said that is because you should know by now that the only woman I want in my life is you and nobody else," he says passionately.

"I know without a shadow of a doubt what I want, and it's standing right here with me. I don't like relationships where I have to guess. Let's just be honest with each other. You know I would never hurt you intentionally. I love you. You are my life. I thank God for you that you have been put into my life."

The words begin to soothe her soul. Her head is hanging in frustration, but he lifts it gently with his hand, wiping the tears from her face. "It's you and me. We're in this thing together, all the way to the end," he says.

She looks at him and places her head in the middle of his chest, trying to lose her very self in the security of his love for her. With her head still in the middle of his chest and with her hands on small of his back, she says, "I am so sorry, Craig. Please forgive me. I apologize for all of this drama that I am causing with our wedding date being so close."

"It's all right, angel. Maybe I should have shared with you more about my past relationships, just in case. But I just don't like dragging old baggage into new areas of my life," he says.

Craig puts his arm around her, and they start walking toward the elevator with all of her stuff in hand.

"I hope you didn't forget that we still have to go by your parents' house for dinner," Craig says while taking the bag and books out of her arms.

"I almost forgot, and we have to get a dessert of some sort to bring to the dinner," she responds.

He presses the button to the elevator and then leans on the wall. She starts taking her hair down, running her fingers through it. He looks on in with an intense stare. She catches him looking at her. "What are you looking at?" she asks, smiling.

"I am looking at what's mine, that's what," he says jokingly.

The elevator door opens, and they enter. He rests against the wall, showing his obvious fatigue. She walks up to him and presses herself up against him. "Legally, I am not yours yet," she says, softly kissing him on his lips and then rubbing her lip gloss off his lips with her thumb. He licks his lips, turning red.

A few moments later in the parking lot of the hospital, Rebecca says, "I am going to go to the store. You go ahead to the house and get changed too because it is suppose to be kind of casual. If you knew how my mom is, you'd come prepared. I will see you there shortly. Okay, babe?" she says, giving instructions.

"That's cool. I have my slacks, tie, shirt, and blazer in the car, so I am all set," he says confidently, kissing her on the cheek and putting her in her truck.

Once having helped her into the car, he waits for her to start up and pull off while sitting in his car. They part ways to meet up at Pastor Washington's house.

Twenty-five minutes later Craig has made it to the Washingtons' house in Germantown. Parked outside on their estate, he prays, "Lord please let everything go right for tonight." He begins to think on the fact that since they have gotten engaged they really haven't had a chance to sit down with the family. "Please go before me, Lord, and give me favor. In Jesus's name, amen."

While he finishes praying, Rebecca pulls up behind him. He gets out of his car with a smile plastered across his face. She gets out and then reaches back in the truck and pulls out the cake and walks over to him. Craig smiles again as she walks up to him. "I don't know how you do it, girl. You just look beautiful all the time, and you are looking especially good right now in that dress."

"Well, thank you, honey," she says in her Southern belle voice. "You look great too, but let me fix a few things on you."

He looks at her in confusion. She places the cake on the top of the car. "You don't need this," she says, taking his tie off and straightening his blazer as well. "Now, that's better. It doesn't look like you are trying so hard," she says, laughing.

They walk up to the porch of the house with the night surrounding them like a cloak, but the lights within the landscaping light the way. She can see that he is a little nervous.

"Just relax, baby. You look good enough to eat. They already love you because I love you. It will be fine," she says.

Rebecca reassures him by giving him a quick kiss and then rings the doorbell. Anthony, her little brother, opens up the door. "What's up, guys? What took ya'll so long?" he asks.

"Boy, hush. Please evaporate somewhere," she replies.

"Whatever!" Anthony says playfully.

"What's up, man? I am her younger brother. It is good to meet you," Anthony says, pulling Craig in from outside into the foyer area of the house, shaking his hand and pulling him into a hug.

"It's good to meet you too, Anthony," Craig replies.

"Momma!" Big head here!" Anthony says. Rebecca pushes him.

"Would you please go somewhere, pest?"

Mother Washington makes her way to the foyer to greet them. Passing Anthony, she smacks him on his shoulder, telling him to behave, and shakes her head. Rebecca turns to him and checks him out one last time, looking at his lips to make sure there is not a trace of lip gloss on them from her.

Mother Washington comes up to them, looking graceful and sharp, as she always does. "Hey, both of you. I am so glad that you could make it tonight with your busy schedules and all," she says as she hugs both of them. "We are all in the family room talking together," she says, leading them to the family room in the house. "Your father has been asking where you two were."

"Yeah, I am sure that he has been," Rebecca replies.

They reach the family room where Pop Washington is sitting back, relaxed in his chair, and see Paige and her husband and children are there. As Rebecca and Craig make their entrance, the twins immediately run up to their Auntie Rebe, hugging her legs. "Hey, Auntie!" says both of the twins.

"Hey, babies. How have my babies been doing?" she says, bending down to hug them.

Craig goes over to greet Pop Washington, putting his hand out. "It's always a pleasure, sir, to see you," he says.

"It's good to see you too. Have a seat, son," Pop Washington replies.

The room is filled with comfortable lighting that would make anyone feel welcome and scents of home cooking. Before they can sit down, Mother Washington comes back at the entrance of the family room, informing everyone that it's time to eat.

"Girls, I need you in the kitchen so you can help bring out the food to the dining table," Mom says, beckoning them to follow her. The men and children head to the dining room while the ladies head to the kitchen. "Well, looks like your man is comfortable around us," Paige comments smugly.

"Why wouldn't he be?" Rebecca asks.

"Well, you know, ya'll are so busy all the time. We just don't see as much of you as we used to," Paige says as they enter into the kitchen.

As Paige goes to a dish on the counter, she says, "You know I am your big sista. We haven't really had all that much time to really get to know him like we want."

Mom Washington looks over at Paige. "All right now, Paige," she says authoritatively.

"What, Momma? I am not starting anything," she says with the tray in her hands, going out into the dining room.

Rebecca looks over at her mother, still standing in the kitchen. Rebecca takes a serving dish in her hands as well. "I am telling you, Momma, Paige and I may be close, but she better not start tonight, or I will finish it," she says before she walks out, heading to the dining room.

A few minutes later, the ladies have finished bringing the food to the dining table. The ladies take their seats, and they all join hands, and Pop Washington offers a prayer of blessing over the food they are about to eat.

"So, since we don't really get to talk much, with sista being so busy and all, are you guys excited about the wedding? Have you been able to get a lot of things done?" Paige says in a snide tone, holding her head to the side, looking at Becca and then Craig.

Rebecca, irritated with the gesture and comment, doesn't respond. Craig looks at her, feeling her irritation, and speaks up. "Well, despite how busy we are at the hospital, we always try to make time for each other to ensure everything is moving ahead smoothly. We went ahead and found this great wedding coordinator that will be taking care of everything else for us, so angel can concentrate on her studies for school."

That catches Father Washington's attention. "School? What do you mean school?" he asks.

Rebecca coughs on her food and hits Craig on his thigh. He looks surprised and says softly, "I am sorry, babe. Was I not supposed to say anything?"

Mother Washington interrupts at the other end of the table. "Becca, is there something you need to tell us?"

"Well, Momma, I was going to tell you guys later, but Craig blurted it out before I could say something," she says, hitting him with the back of her hand on his arm.

"What? Sorry," Craig says with a chuckle.

"I was offered a full ride to go to medical school to become a full-fledged doctor. Can you believe it? I am going to be a doctor," she says with excitement in her voice.

"Are you serious?" Pop Washington asks.

"My little princess is going to be a doctor. Praise the Lord; God is just awesome," Mom Washington says with a big smile on her face and hand on top of her chest.

"How in the world are you going to be able to balance that all? You barely have time for your family now. We have to get an appointment just to see you. How do you think you're going to be a successful wife and mother with all of that on your plate?" Paige says.

Paige looks at Rebecca and then her mom and dad, ignoring Craig. Paige's husband, Tyler, interjects, telling her that it's not her place to say something like that. Paige strongly comes back at her husband.

"Wait a minute. Hold up," Rebecca says strongly.

"All right, girls. That's enough," Pop Washington says sternly.

Craig looks at Rebecca, shaking his head, hoping that she would not get into it with her sister.

"No, I need to address this," she says as she places her fork by her plate. "Just what is your problem exactly, Paige? I really don't understand. I really didn't want to go there with you, but you have been kind of off for a while with me, and I don't understand. I've been trying to figure it out and be cordial, but that ain't gonna work, I see."

Paige cuts her off with a very distinct attitude.

"There is nothing wrong with me, okay. And if there were, you don't have the time to even go into it anyway and figure it out," Paige says.

"No, you did not just go there with me, sista!" Rebecca shouts.

Craig whispers in her ear. "Don't pay any attention to that, angel. It's nothing but the devil, that's all."

"You know what, Paige? I am not going to even entertain what you've just said or dignify that with a response," she says, picking up her glass of iced tea.

Mom Washington starts talking about something else to break the tension in the room between the sisters. Rebecca shakes her head in disbelief at how Paige is acting. "So where is the wedding going to be held? Since we really haven't had a chance to talk about the wedding details," Mom Washington asks.

Craig and Rebecca look at each other. "Well, we wanted to have it at Daddy's church and have him marry us, but then he won't be able to walk me down the aisle if he performs the service," Rebecca explains. "And I want you to walk me down the aisle, Daddy. We kind of figured one of your ministers could do the service for you."

"What about the pastor of the church you attend, Craig? Would he be able to do it?" Pop Washington asks.

"You do still go to church, right? With your oh-so-busy schedule," Paige interjects with plenty of attitude.

"You know what? I have had enough from you, Paige," Rebecca says with her voice pitched high in anger. "You know what? I think you're jealous of me. For once in my life the Lord really is working for me and I am not leaning on you, and you're jealous of that."

Paige tries to interrupt her, but Rebecca shuts her down. "No, shut up! I am talking now. I have the floor. You've done nothing but give attitude since I've gotten engaged. But I know with you it's something bigger than that. I found a man that loves me for me and all I am inside. Most of all, you question our relationship with the Lord. He has shown me the way to the Lord Jesus and his healing. And I saw the Lord through the love that Craig has for me, a love that doesn't judge, push, or put demands on me, but allows me to grow in knowledge, love, and grace. He loves me, just like the Lord, seeing past my faults and imperfections. He's someone I can share my most intimate details and conversations with. This man that God has blessed me with has helped and led me in so many ways, allowing God to use him to minister to me. I truly am sorry, Paige, if you're not happy or if you're jealous or whatever you want to call it. Never once have I questioned your relationship, marriage, or the life that you are living, raising your children and being a wife. I have always looked up to you in many ways and admired that very thing about you. I don't know, sista, if you have not found satisfaction or completion in yourself, life, or marriage, but all I can do is pray for you that you receive what you're looking for," Rebecca finishes and picks up her dinner fork and continues to finish her food as if nothing has happened.

The dining room is silent. Everyone looks at Paige

to comment, but instead she says nothing, her head down with her eyes fixed on the plate in front of her, and finishes eating. Craig and Tyler look around the table with wide eyes.

Then Pop Washington, sitting at the head dining table, breaks the silence with his deep, raspy voice. "Well, how about those football games that came on ESPN last night?"

The men join into the conversation. Once they do, things begin to loosen up again. The rest of the evening continues pleasantly as they discuss plans for the wedding and ministry. Rebecca and Paige didn't speak to each other. Rebecca tried to act like nothing was wrong with her, but it showed on her face.

Late in the evening, it is time for the family to say their good-byes. The house has become a little still. Paige's children are asleep, knocked out in the family room on the couch, and the other set of twins are asleep in their car seats. Craig hugs Mom and Pop Washington, thanking them for the dinner invitation. Rebecca follows, hugging her momma and daddy. "Take care baby girl," Pop says, embracing her.

Mom Washington kisses her on her cheek while Dad Washington is still holding her. "Good night, Becca," Mom says.

Then she goes over to her sister and grabs and embraces her tightly. "You know I love you, sista. Nothing and no one will ever change that," Rebecca says softly into Paige's ear.

Rebecca releases Paige and looks directly in her eyes, but Paige says nothing in response, giving a smirk for a smile. Leaning her head to the side, smiling and shrugging her shoulders, Rebecca turns around and goes out the front door on Craig's arm with both of them saying, "Good night, everyone."

Craig and Rebecca talk as they walk to their cars.

"Man, angel, I am indeed proud and touched by the words you spoke, especially your confession of faith. I have never seen you speak so passionately before about the Lord," Craig says with a big smile on his face.

"Well, you know, something had to be said. I couldn't let her keep disrespecting my man. Plus, everything you have shared with me about love and the love of God had to surface some way," Rebecca replies.

He opens up the door to her truck and puts her in. She starts it up and turns the heat on and lets her window down, seeing that Craig has something else to say.

"You know one thing I think about, though? I hope and pray that you and your sister's relationship isn't hurt over the disagreement tonight," says Craig with concern as he leans over to the window of her truck with his arm on the top of vehicle.

"Sista and I have had many words before that have been a lot harsher than what I said at dinner. We'll be all right. We always are. I guess it's just part of how our relationship is," she says, shrugging her shoulders. "I don't know why. Maybe it's because I have always been the family screw-up for so long, the rebellious one, and now that some things are coming my way, the Lord is blessing me. She might feel like she is being left in the background now, taking backseat instead of being the favorite."

"Oh, I see. Well, angel, you go ahead and get on home. Make sure you call me to let me know you made it home all right. Love you," he says, bidding her good night and kissing her on her forehead.

thirteen

Three weeks have passed by, which have seemed to be never-ending days for Rebecca and Craig, who are anxiously waiting to be united in marriage. So much anticipation has built up dealing with their special day, but especially for Rebecca. It began for her with dreaming of meeting and marrying the man of her dreams and then waking up each morning in her room to harsh reality. She allowed herself to go to any length necessary to get what she was looking for. Now it has come full circle for her. Sitting on the edge of her bed in the new freshness of morning, she begins to think of how far she has come and where God is bringing her. She begins to realize that all this time she was seeking and searching for someone to love and to love her, but first she needed to learn to love herself. She knows her self-worth is in becoming who God has created her to be, and that is a treasure, a jewel to be found and cherished. The steps that it has taken for her to reach where she is have been a difficult road. She thinks of all the bad relationships that she has become involved in, which resulted in the loss of her son. But thinking of these things only causes her to start thanking and praising God for what he has done in her life and how he has brought her through and kept her from losing her mind through it all.

But the God that she had been trained up to know by her parents, who raised her strictly, brought a rift in her life. Just when she was about to throw in the towel after her failed relationships and the loss of her son, God sent her someone who was in sync, not only with her heart and needs, but in accord with the will of God. She figured all this time the man that God had in store for her was right in front of her, but she was too blind to see him, dealing with the affairs of her life and what she wanted to do instead of what God wanted for her.

She thinks, *God is just awesome. Even when we mess something up and miss the mark, he keeps the blessing right in front of us. He sent me a wonderful, God-fearing man to lead me to him at the worst point in my life, when I had no place to go but up. Thank you, God.* Getting up from her bed, she enters the bathroom, humming the wedding march. As she always has done, she stops and looks in the mirror, but today she smiles instead of being overly critical. She thinks of nothing but positive things to say about herself. The glow of happiness is all over her countenance. "It has finally happened for you, girl. Not only did you get blessed with a great man, but you were blessed with a man that led to find love in yourself and the Lord as well. Thank you,

Jesus!" she says loudly with a humongous smile on her face and joy in her heart and soul. Rebecca does a little dance around the bathroom, still looking in the mirror. She goes over and turns on the shower water. The house phone rings while she checks the temperature of the water. Going over to the phone, she presses the speaker button in order to answer the phone. "Hello?" Rebecca says.

"Somebody sounds happy," the male voice on the other end speaks softly.

"Don't try and disguise your voice with me, honey," she says in a playful voice, looking at her ring finger. "I know it's you," she says, laughing. "How are you doing this morning, baby?"

"I am doing good. I am floating on air, angel, floating on air. I get to marry and spend the rest of my life with my best friend," Craig says.

Rebecca leans up against the marble vanity, smiling and biting her bottom lip. "Oh, really?" she says flirtatiously.

"Yes, really," he responds. "Whatcha doing?"

"The usual. You know, baby, having do my little morning regimen to make sure I am fresh and ready to go. I have to brush my hair, shower, and all the other little stuff, you know, putting on the finishing touches on everything before I get to country club," she explains, looking at the time.

Craig sighs. "Well, angel, I am not going to hold you long on the phone. I just wanted to hear your voice this morning.

"Before we get off the phone, I want us to touch

and agree and pray over this day, that God go before us and that his presence will be in the midst of us," he says.

With those very words that he spoke, something stirred down in the pit of her soul, which caused her to have even more respect for him, knowing that she has made the right choice, allowing him to lead her and be over her as a covering.

"All right, sweetie, go ahead. I am ready," Rebecca says.

Craig begins the prayer. "Father, in the name of Jesus, we just glorify you right now for the life you have given us, Lord, just for even the blood that you shed on the cross for us, most of all, giving us each other to glorify you. We ask that you go before us today and bless it, Lord, and bless this union that we are about to enter into. We love you and bless you. In Jesus's name, amen."

Warm tears roll down Rebecca's face as she feels not only the spirit of sincerity but his love for her and the Lord as well.

"Thank you, baby. I needed that this morning," she says.

"Well, I am going to let you go so you can continue to get ready. I will see you at the rendezvous point," Craig says with a chuckle in his voice.

Hanging up the phone, she feels so good on the inside from what she has heard from Craig this morning. She thinks, *Is this really real, or could this be a dream where everything is falling in place the way that I have always imagined it?*

Half an hour later, the doorbell rings. Rebecca quickly makes it to the door. She opens the door, and Grace and Paige come in. Paige begins to inform her of everything that is going on with all the festivities.

"Sista, I have already spoken with the wedding coordinator, Melody. She says everything is running on schedule. She is just awaiting our arrival," Paige says.

"Take that worried look off your face, sista. It's nothing for you to worry about. This is your day. Don't obsess; just be happy today," Paige says, checking behind Rebecca to make sure that she has all of her items before they leave the house.

Opening the refrigerator, Grace says, "Girl, I am hungry right now. What you got to eat in this fridge?"

"There's some fruit, to snack on in there, I believe," Rebecca says, looking at her watch again.

"Don't worry about the time, Becky. Everything is waiting on us; the stylists and everything are at your beck and call," Grace says with a giggle.

Then Rebecca's cell phone rings. Paige picks it up, checking the caller ID to see who is calling. Rebecca asks her who's calling.

"It's Momma," Paige says in response.

She answers the phone to make sure everything is all right. "Where are you girls at?" Mom Washington inquires.

"We are trying to get her out of the house now, Momma. We will be there shortly," Paige responds.

"Please hurry up because this wedding coordinator is getting on my nerves, making sure that everything is running minute by minute," Mother Washington says with agitation in her voice.

Paige rolls her eyes and responds, "Yes, Mother. We are trying to get her out the door now."

As they walk out the front door, they see the white limousine parked outside. As Paige hangs up the phone, Rebecca asks, "What did Momma want?"

"Trying to see if we had already left because the wedding coordinator is getting on her nerves," Paige responds.

"I can't believe I am getting married today," Rebecca says once they're in the limo.

Grace and Paige look at her kind of strangely. "Just think, girl, you almost missed that," Grace says with a chuckle.

"You know, you're right. I was just thinking about all of that this morning," Rebecca says.

"What are you guys talking about?" Paige asks with a clueless look on her face.

"Well, you know with me and my issues, dealing with Jacob and Philip. That very same man who I am ready to walk beside waited for me and stuck by me through all of that drama that I had going on in my life," Rebecca says, smiling.

A look of disappointment comes over Paige's countenance, and a tear rolls down her cheek as she looks out the window.

"Sista, what's wrong?" Rebecca asks. "If anybody should be crying, it should be me," she says with a giggle.

Paige turns her head from the window, looks

intently at Rebecca, and grabs her hand. Rebecca thinks, *Lord, what is my sister getting ready to say? Please don't let it be something to ruin my day.*

Paige begins to speak, swallowing first. "Um ... I really want to say I am so sorry, Sis. I want to apologize about my outburst some weeks ago. I want our relationship to be like it was before, even better."

"Apologize for what?" Rebecca asks with a look of concern.

"Well, for how I behaved and all that transpired between us at the family dinner," Paige says.

"That was a few weeks ago, Paige. I haven't really thought about that anymore. I mean, I figured our relationship might change, and it may not because we are sisters and have been through worse," Rebecca answers, trying to keep her composure.

Grace tries to interrupt to keep peace, feeling that there might be some type of conflict. "Paige, sweetie, do you think we should be talking about this right now while we are on our way to the country club?" She reaches over and places her hand on Paige's knee, suggesting that she cut the conversation off where it was going.

"I have to do this or I won't feel right inside. And I want to better with my relationship with my sister. At that get-together at Momma's house, you were right of my being jealous of you," Paige says.

Rebecca is shocked at the confession. Usually Paige never confesses when she is wrong.

"I am so used to being the one that is there for Momma and Daddy, the one that didn't make mistakes, the one that had all the attention because I felt I was doing right," Paige continues as she holds Rebecca's hand.

Tears begin to run down Rebecca's cheeks as she intently listens to Paige's confession and apology.

"I was so used to you making all the mistakes, and then once God truly blessed you with a relationship with him and a man after his own heart and yours, I began to get jealous instead of celebrating you."

"Why would you get jealous, sista? You have been my inspiration for a family," she says, sobbing.

"I guess I got so wrapped up in being a preacher's wife for Tyler and all the congregation and being a mother to my children that I kind of lost myself in all of it. Then I saw what you have accomplished and how you grown, not just as a woman, but also as a lady of grace and a woman of God too. You know me, sista. I just started hating on you, plain and simple. I want to say I am truly sorry, and would you please forgive me for my stupidness?" Paige says, crying as well.

Rebecca looks at her. "Of course I forgive you, sista," she says, pulling her close and embracing her. Then she laughs. "Lord, I am glad we got all of this out before we put any makeup on because it would have been all over the place. Even look at Grace there; she's crying too."

"We need to let some windows down in here because it is getting hot with all this crying," Grace responds with a laugh. Rebecca and her sister continue to wipe their eyes using a handkerchief.

Grace comments, "You know, it is not very often

that you see sisters mending their relationships with each other, restoring a bond that has been broken between family. Usually there is competition, strife, and envy instead of love and unity."

"We are not going to be any good when we get there," Rebecca says, laughing again.

Rebecca looks out the window for a moment to ponder a few things. *Well, I guess that is a weight that has been lifted. I don't have to deal with it anymore. My relationship is right with my sista. I can move on to something else and enjoy being united with my husband to be. Lord, let it be everything I envision. Most of all, I pray you are pleased by this.*

Before they know it, the limo has arrived at the country club. "We're here, girl," Grace says loudly. This brings her out of the moment of reflection.

"Oh, we are here already. All right, let's do this," Rebecca says as the limo driver opens her door for her to get out. They quickly make their way into the country club through the double-door entrance. They find the wedding coordinator waiting on them.

"You made it in good time. What in the world? Your face is a little puffy; you must have been crying, but that is all right. We have the technicians here to help with that," Melody says, beckoning Rebecca to follow her.

"Everything is so beautiful and elegant, just the way I pictured it. Oh my God," Rebecca comments with her hand to her chest, in awe at how beautifully decorated the country club was.

Before she follows the wedding coordinator, Melody, she looks at the different flower arrangements, delicately placed fabrics with colors of purple and burgundy. The sitting area for the ceremony was masterfully arranged, set diagonally in two sections, allowing for the bride's processional and the bridal party to march. The other side of the club area sectioned off. Set to the back of the club are the tables where guests and the bridal party will sit. The sight just seems surreal to her. Just taking it all in, the grandeur of affair brings her to tears again. *I just can't believe it. I am breathless and in complete awe. God is just good.*

Grace and Melody step over and place their hands on her back. Rebecca turns to Melody. "I just can't believe it. It's beautiful. I am without words. You did an awesome job, Melody," Rebecca says, embracing her.

"Thanks so much, Becky. I am so glad you're happy with everything. But now, it is time for us to get you up here with the rest of your bridesmaids to get your hair and everything else done so we can get you into your wedding dress," Melody says as she guides her to the stairs.

"Where is my mother?" Rebecca says.

"She is up there with the rest of the wedding party," Melody says in response.

"Lord knows she is probably driving those women up the wall, trying to make sure everything is just perfect," Paige says jokingly.

The four of them make their way up to the prep room. When Rebecca opens the door, Mom Washington greets her with a hug and kiss.

"My baby girl is getting married today. Thank you, Jesus," she says, doing a little dance after hugging her.

Rebecca walks over to her chair where her stylist is waiting on her and sits down, letting out a huge breath. Her stylist greets her and asks if her style will be the same as she had chosen before. "Yes. I am in your hands, girl. Do your thang," Rebecca says as she crosses her legs and sits back in the chair.

"Momma, have you seen my babies?" Paige asks while getting her hair fixed too.

"I saw them, honey. They look good and put together. Tyler did a good job of dressing them," Mother Washington replies.

"Has anyone seen my man?" Rebecca inquires with a huge smile on her face.

One of the bridesmaids answers, "They have been locked up in that other room. Craig's dad and your dad have been keeping them in line and getting them together over there."

"You know, he was trying to make his way over here to make sure he saw you when you got here, but I told the men to put him on lockdown," Mom says, laughing.

"Lord, I am so nervous. I don't know what to do. I feel a little sick to my stomach," Rebecca says.

Grace smiles, shaking her head. "Becky, you'll be all right, girl. It's nothing but wedding day excitement and jitters. Can somebody please get my sister a little Alka-Seltzer," Grace says.

"I think every woman gets it right before the actual ceremony. You know, you finally are going to have him on lockdown," Paige says, smiling and doing a little demonstration.

Their laughter helps to ease Rebecca's jitters. *Lord, just let me keep it together, please. Just keep it together so I won't be a mess.*

A few hours later everything is almost ready. Rebecca comes into the room with the bridesmaids, who ooh and ahh at her beauty and grace. Immediately, her mom, sister, and friend Grace break down in tears, trying to dab their eyes to keep their mascara from running.

Her mom comes over to her, gazes, and nods her head in approval. "I am just so proud of you, Becca. I am really without words right now. You're a vision of beauty. Truly God's light is shining down on you this day. I love you, Becca. Continue to be who you are and be true to yourself and let God do the rest," Mom says, giving a little speech.

Waiting until Mom Washington finishes, Melody gets everyone's attention. "All right, ladies. It is time to start. Mother of the bride and bridesmaids, your escorts are waiting for you at the bottom of the stairs. Be graceful as you go down the steps, place your arm on his, and march to the front on beat with the processional music."

The ladies start to march down the steps as directed. Rebecca is waiting at the back until all have marched; then, after all the ladies have made it down the steps to their escorts and made it to the front, Melody looks at her. "It's time," she says with a smile on her face. *Take a breath and exhale, girl. Relax, release, and take your time down these steps,* Rebecca thinks to herself. As the wedding song plays, she strolls down the steps slowly, seeing her father at the bottom waiting on her with his hand holding the lapel of his tuxedo, looking dapper. She smiles, seeing her father waiting for her with a proud look on his face.

Making it to the bottom of the step, she takes her dad's arm. He leans in to kiss her cheek. "You look like an angel, my dear. You look beautiful and radiant," he says.

Smiling, she bows her head for just a second and looks at Pop Washington.

"You ready, Daddy?" she asks, making eye contact.

"I sure am, princess. You ready?" he replies. She nods, and they proceed to march to the destination where her future is, filled with promise and purpose. Her eyes are fixed on Craig, down at the end of the aisle. She finally makes it to Craig, who is quick to take her hand from her dad. The wedding guests see his eagerness to receive his bride, and there is a little laughter through the audience. The preacher begins to perform the ceremony, but he lets the audience know that they in turn wanted to say some things along with their vows.

"I thank God for this moment of being here with you, who trusted God and followed me to our destiny of being together. I know this one thing that I desire and that our love will continue to grow stronger in God and love each other until the end of time," Craig says, holding her hands and looking into her eyes.

"My heart beats for you, my love. You won my heart so that God could win my soul. I am grateful for your undying loving for me. As God loves me without limits, so have you. Your finger was on the pulse of God to know what this woman wanted, desired, and needed. Thank you. I will love you until the end of my days," she says with tears in her eyes, trying to hold them back.

The minister asks for their rings, praying the blessing over them, and he instructs them to present their rings to each other with the vow over the rings. He then announces that they are now husband and wife and tells Craig he may kiss his new bride. Craig lifts up her veil. Rebecca is smiling and bouncing a little, awaiting the kiss from her husband. He pulls her gently to him and kisses her passionately. Now the tears that she has fought so long are rolling down her cheeks. Once they have stopped kissing, the minister announces, "I'd like to present to everyone Dr. and Mrs. Craig Lowe." Everyone claps and stands for their processional back down the aisle together, shouting, whistling, yelling, and head for the celebration of their union together.

The festivities begin in the country club. All Rebecca can feel down is overwhelming joy, not just the joy of being married, but also the everlasting joy of God's promise and purpose being fulfilled in her life.

EPILOGUE

Two years have passed. Rebecca has become an intern now at the hospital and is doing her residency from the opportunity that was provided to her. Craig and Rebecca are still together. They have encountered some challenges within their two years of being together, just as every couple does, but they count their blessings of having each other. They continue to realize that in their marriage that God has given them each other. The marriage didn't come as a prepackaged present with everything in there, but they know the present box is empty and they have to fill it with their love, trust, memories, and every other thing that comes with the marriage, good and bad. Knowing that it takes two to make it work, realizing that God is the center and the fore focus of their love and relationship together as they love God together. Seeing that the two years have passed, Craig has suggested that they start talking about children, which Rebecca is open to, though she still thinks of the one child that was lost from her tragic miscarriage.

Am I up for the challenge of having another child, knowing what my body went through? But with the love I have for my husband, how could I deny him of such a gift that God could bring through me, she thinks to herself. Craig doesn't push the issue of children but is sensitive to her feelings of knowing how bad it was for her to lose the child that she had.

With this new challenge before her, she prays that the Lord's will is done. If the Lord wants her to have more children, she would not deny herself or her husband the joy of bringing another life into the world. One day while at the hospital, Rebecca is just finishing her shift for the day and runs into Grace.

"Hey, Becky. How are you doing? Haven't been able to catch up with you with the way our schedules are," says Grace.

"I have been doing fine, just a little more tired than usual today. I am getting ready to get something to snack on before I go to the house because I know my love is waiting on me at home," Rebecca says, smiling.

Grace walks with her to the vending machine in the waiting area where the guest lounge is located. "Becky, marriage is agreeing with you, though. You look so full, like you're about to burst," Grace says, giggling.

"Girl, these cycles that I have been having have been a little different to where I am retaining more water, like I am picking up some weight. I don't know what it is," Rebecca says as she shrugs her shoulders, bending down to get a sweet out of the vending machine, and she stands back up. She gets dizzy and has to catch hold of Grace.

"Whoa there, girl. Are you okay?" Grace comments with a look of concern.

"Yeah, I am all right. I must have stood up too quick or something," Rebecca replies, trying to shake it off, walking with Grace.

As they continue to walk down the corridor of the hospital passageway, she continues to look at Rebecca.

"Becky, are you sure you're okay? You look kind of funny now," Grace says.

"Do I?" she asks.

"I am probably just tired, that is all, trying to get home after this long shift. These cramps are extreme too, I tell you," Rebecca says, grabbing her stomach as she walks.

Continuing to the elevator in the brightly lit passageway, she puts her hand on the wall.

"These cramps are getting on my nerves. I could slap somebody," Rebecca says, looking very disturbed.

"When was the last time you had a checkup, girl?" Grace asks.

Rebecca thinks, *Lord, I have been too busy with work and stuff at home with Craig. I don't even remember my last checkup.*

"Maybe you ought to call and get you an appointment or just pop in to the OB/GYN office so they can you look you over, because you know sometimes when your cycles get like that it could be fibroid cysts that make your cycles like that. I know; I've had them. They make a cycle seem unbearable," Grace says as she places her hand on her belly in sympathetic response.

As the elevator doors break open with the sound of the bell, they hug and go their separate ways with Rebecca entering into the elevator. Rebecca looks in the shining reflection of the elevator doors and turns to the side, looking at the bottom of her stomach by pulling the scrub shirt tight to her body, looking and examining, thinking how women are very prone to having fibroid cyst tumors. *My belly does seem a little bit bigger now. To me, it looks more like water weight retention. It can't be those tumors. I pray it is not that in Jesus's name,* she thinks to herself for a moment. Knowing the information as a seasoned nurse, now doctor, she gets in her mind that she wants to check it out. A bell sound is made by the elevator again as the doors open. She exits with the intention of finding an exam room with an ultrasound machine to check to make sure that there is no mass on or in her uterus, causing her cycles to be a little unusual.

Not really wanting to have to be told by another doctor any bad news or even share what's going on with anyone, she finds a quiet, empty room with an ultrasound machine in it and closes the door. Placing her bag on the top of the examination bed, she pulls the machine close to the bed and sits down on the stool the doctors sit on, turning the machine on. Lifting the bottom of her mauve-colored scrubs shirt and reaching in the drawer to get the examining tissue cover paper to tuck into her pants just under her belly, she takes a swallow and then exhales with a sigh of worry, which seems so loud to her that it echoes through the quiet room. Taking the clear ultrasound jelly, she spreads it over her lower abdomen. Then she picks up the wand to the machine and proceeds to place it on her belly. Even though the room is cold and quiet, she begins to have little beads of sweat pop on her forehead. *Come on now; you can do this. It's better you find out for yourself and then get a second opinion if it is something odd,* she thinks to herself. Placing the wand on her belly, she starts on the top of abdomen right where the navel is and then proceeds down. She then hears the strangest sound, which shocks her, and she drops the ultrasound wand in her lap. She thinks, *This is crazy. Did I hear just what I thought I heard?* Picking the wand up again, she places it on there and hears the sound ever so clearly and looks at the screen and sees not one string of pearls, not two, but three. What was she looking at on the screen? To her shock and amazement, thrice a blessing wrapped up tight in her womb, nestled in the comfort of God's blessing of purpose and promise of his destiny for her life.

How could this be possible and I not know? Rebecca thinks. Then what comes to mind is what her mother spoke as encouragement to her in the loss of her son. *Give me the first, your first son, and take my comfort for your dark times, for I have something in store for you that is an overflow.* She calls back to her remembrance the conversation with her mother. Feeling this overwhelming flow of God's blessing is more than she could ever hope for, knowing it was not in her control but God's. A praise bubbles on the inside as she sits in the room, praising God, ready to share her news. Excited about what she has discovered, she pulls her phone out and calls Craig. In talking with him, she lets him know that she had some good news to share. Quite naturally she leads him to think that it's about her job, but then she springs the news on him. "Honey, you'll never believe it, but I am pregnant!" she says with a shout of excitement.

A SPECIAL NOTE OF ENCOURAGEMENT

The battle that we often have with our relationships is trying to figure out on our own whom we should be with. Leaning and trusting in our intelligence leads us to many of the pitfalls and mistakes that occur in our lives. Low self-esteem can drive a person throughout life. It can drive us in so many ways that it takes our lives in different directions. When you have low self-esteem, it pushes you to make certain choices. It makes you accept what God didn't have in store for you. Attaching ourselves to bad soul ties takes our lives down a path and direction that God didn't mean for us to go in, taking us into dark places that we can't escape or recover from, unable to see the light of God. Not having a relationship with God puts us in a terrible predicament to sometimes just accept anything. Bad relationships spiral our lives into destruction, which God did not have in store for us.

Although many capably deal with being single parents, as my mother did, raising two children on her own, it's just not something you should have to face alone, without the help of the one that you thought you would be with for the rest of your life. Remember and realize that the love of the almighty Father is always there for us, to hold us and take us through every facet of life.

The one thing that the devil has tried to plan out and strategically set up for us is destruction, just like Rebecca, who tried to run from different issues in her life, searching for answers but not really going to God, who is the source and has all knowledge. She dealt with the issue of abandonment because, even though both father and mother were present, they were not really there emotionally. They were so tied up in the church work and various affairs dealing with members that they did not spend enough time creating solid and truthful relationships with their children, having that true family time together. That is one thing that we have to be so careful of in today's society, looking at our children and the adults they have grown up to be or will be. Those who are neglected will end up with no family values and no relationship with God. When a family makes time for family talks and play times, shares affection, and teaches good sibling relationships, it teaches how to be more social and have good relationships and good self-esteem as well.

The purpose and promise of God's blessing is what he wants to release in our very lives, despite the various ups and downs and the seesaw effects that reoccur in our lives from day to day. As people, we know that the things we have orchestrated, some stuff we have sown will come around again in order to be dealt with in some type of way, but it's nothing that God can't get you through. God our Father rains on the just as well as the unjust. He is rich and great in mercy when we heed to the call of his plan, purpose, promise, and salvation.

Depression, we see, comes in so many different forms and disguises. If we are not careful to really cleave to the Lord when we encounter life's hurdles, the devil, our enemy, will try to bring a spirit of depression along with oppression. Sometimes in our lives we may experience the loss of something so dear and close to us, it could rock the very foundations of our world and faith, but with God's Word, knowledge, faith, clarity, and seasoned Christians in place, they can help pull us out of the dark times and prepare us for the destiny and promise that is ahead of us. Don't get lost in the worst season of your life. Remember, seasons change. This too shall pass. Weeping may endure for a night, but joy comes in the morning. The darkest hour is just before the break of day. Sometimes the picture and the outlook are distorted because the dust has not settled yet, so as you get closer to the promise or the blessing, refocus on what God has planned and destined for you.

To some of you, who may have everything you want materially but are missing that love and companionship that you long for because of your self-esteem, brokenness, or different kind of relationships, whether it be family or friends, God has the remedy for whatever situation it may be. Sanctified and suffering, you may feel you have needs that are not being fulfilled physically and mentally, but I recommend that you stop looking and searching for love in all the wrong faces and places. Don't have your passion misplaced, looking to only the physical when it can only be fulfilled through the Lord Jesus. Remember,